W9-CAM-038

THE MYSTERY OF
THE BLINKING EYE

Trixie Belden

Your TRIXIE BELDEN Library

Trixie Belden and the
MYSTERY OF
THE BLINKING EYE

BY KATHRYN KENNY

Cover by Jack Wacker

GOLDEN PRESS
Western Publishing Company, Inc.
Racine, Wisconsin

CONTENTS

THE MYSTERY OF
THE BLINKING EYE

A Strange Beginning • 1

TRIXIE BELDEN, fourteen, hurried from the taxicab that had taken her and her friends to Kennedy International Airport in New York City. Her sandy curls, damp from the heat of midsummer, clung tightly to her head, like a cap.

"I'm just sure I heard the flight from Chicago announced," she called back to her older brother Brian. "Hurry and pay the driver, please?"

"I've already charged the cab to Daddy," Trixie's best friend Honey Wheeler said. "Daddy gave Jim and me a credit card. You don't need to be in such a hurry, Trixie. Wait for the rest of us! It'll take half an hour for the passengers to get up here after the plane has landed."

"Gosh, yes," Trixie's other brother, Mart, added. "The way you're rushing, Trixie, anyone'd think one of the astronauts had just landed from the moon."

"You *know* Bob and Barbara and Ned have never been in New York before," Trixie said, but she slowed down. "I don't want them to be worried if they don't find us. Kennedy International Airport is acres bigger than the Des Moines airport, and it's almost as busy as the one in Chicago, where they made connections."

"You seem to forget that Ned is the same age as Brian and I," Honey's adopted brother, Jim, said, laughing indulgently. He never really seemed upset at anything Trixie did or said. "A person seventeen can take care of himself."

"Yeah," Mart said. "Bob and Barbara are fifteen, like me, so Bob's no baby, either."

"I suppose you're right," Trixie admitted a little shamefacedly, "but anyway I want to be right on hand to welcome them. Isn't it wonderful that they are finally coming to visit here?"

"I'll say it is," Dan Mangan said. He was the only member of their club, Bob-Whites of the Glen, who hadn't gone to Happy Valley Farm in Iowa at Easter time, so he didn't know the Hubbell twins, Barbara and Bob, or Ned Schulz. "I'm glad I'm finally going to have a chance to meet them. Don't think I wasn't envious of the good times you had there when I was studying hard back in Sleepyside. Even if I did make up my grades so I could stay in the same class with Jim and Brian, the two brains, I still wish I could have been with you. Say, look at the bulletin board! You *didn't* hear the announcement of the plane's arrival, Trixie. It's going to be an hour late." Dan settled on a bench and panted exaggeratedly. "You and all your hurrying, Trix!"

"Boy, do we always follow Trixie like a pack of geese!" Mart said and plopped down beside Dan. "Why do we always pirouette to her peremptory Pied Piper piping?"

"Just listen to him!" Diana Lynch said, her violet eyes widening. "Isn't he smart?"

Mart loved to use big words. He usually knew what he was saying, too. Trixie was proud of his knowledge, though she didn't often let him know it.

All of the group were pupils at Sleepyside Junior-Senior High, and their club, the Bob-Whites of the Glen, had been formed primarily to help with fund-raising for various projects—UNICEF, crippled children, earthquake sufferers, and many private charities. The fact that these activities always seemed to go hand in hand with mysterious happenings was quite by accident. The same mysterious happenings offered Trixie and Honey an opportunity to get in some good practice for what they hoped would be their serious lifework, the Belden-Wheeler Detective Agency.

Just now, though, with their friends from Iowa expected momentarily, the Bob-Whites had no objective in mind for the next few days other than to have a wonderful time together exploring in the big city of New York.

The Iowans expected, after a few days in New York, to go on to Maine to visit relatives, then to stay awhile in Sleepyside.

Mr. Wheeler, Honey and Jim's father, was very wealthy and commuted daily to his business from their home, Manor House, in Sleepyside. He kept a large apartment in New York to entertain business friends and so he and Mrs. Wheeler could stay overnight when attending the theater or opera.

Now he had turned the apartment over to the young people. Because there would be ten of them, he had arranged for additional quarters across the hall. Miss Trask, the Wheeler housekeeper, would stay in the apartment with the dual purpose of acting as chaperon and visiting her sister who was an invalid in a New York hospital.

"I wish we were going to be in Sleepyside instead of spending all this time in the city," Dan said. "From what you tell me, Bob's a neat pitcher, and we have some good games coming up in our league."

"Maybe he can do that later," Trixie said. "They're so excited, all three of them, at the prospect of seeing New York. I never get over being thrilled with it myself."

"I *love* New York!" Diana exclaimed. "I love to walk down Fifth Avenue and stop in all the fabulous stores. The clothes there are dreamy!"

"I wonder if Bob and Ned are coming this far just to see clothes," Mart said dryly. "I doubt it."

"It's part of the glamour, and Barbara will like it,"

Honey said. "There are thousands of other things to see and do."

"They won't be able to see much in a few days."

"Maybe not, Mart. Do you remember, though, what Daddy said to those men who were in Sleepyside for his bankers' convention? He told them if they stayed a week in New York, they'd see everything; if they stayed a month, they'd see *some* things they wanted to see; but if they intended to live in the city, they'd never see *anything*."

"I doubt if a person could see all he wanted to see in New York in a lifetime," Honey said. "Things change so. What are you looking at, Trixie?"

"That woman sitting on the bench near the door. I noticed her when we came in. I think she's in some kind of trouble."

"Oh, no!" Mart wailed. "Not again! Trixie, if you get us into one of your mystery messes and spoil our New York fun. . . ."

"I think she's terribly upset," Trixie went on, paying no attention to her brother.

"Darned if she isn't," Jim said. "Trixie, do you think you might be able to help her?"

Trixie was halfway across the room, with Honey and Diana not far behind her. They stood aside and waited, however, while Trixie sat down next to the foreign-looking woman and took her hand. "Is something wrong?" she asked. "Can I help you?"

The gray-haired woman wearing a black dress took a big handkerchief from a crumpled red cotton bag and mopped her face. "I lost!" she wailed. "I miss plane I supposed to take. To Mexico City. Oh, miss, what I do? No friends. No money. In Mexico City my daughter wait, and maybe I no come. What I do? Everyone look at me. No one help." The woman's shoulders shook, and she raised her face pitifully to Trixie.

"Maybe there is something I can do. Tell me about it," Trixie said.

"I visit my cousin in this big city. I tell fortunes. I *not* a crook. Police say I crook and have to get out. I not know how to tell them they wrong. My cousin ran away from me. She afraid of police. I afraid, too. I buy ticket to my home in Mexico City, spend all my money, come here to wait for airplane. It never come. I ask at window. They tell me go someplace else. I not understand. Where *is* right place? I wait so long; now I miss plane."

"Let me take your ticket. I'll find out," Trixie said. She went to the information booth inside the entrance and found that there was still time for the woman to make the flight and that she should be in the *Aeronaves de Mexico* terminal, near the Van Wyck Expressway, instead of in the TWA flight center.

"My friends and I will take you right to the gate where you should be. You haven't missed your plane. Come with us."

Trixie motioned to the other Bob-Whites to join her. When they did so, the woman looked about, frightened. "So many people?" she asked.

"They are my friends. We are all your friends."

"I no like too many people. I no like all these boys. I like you. I trust you. I stay here till they go away."

"Then I'll go with you alone," Trixie told her. "We'll get the shuttle bus." She took the woman's bundle and helped her to her feet. "I'll be back in plenty of time to meet the Chicago plane," she told the Bob-Whites.

Jim held up his thumb and index finger in a circle to tell her "Okay!"

It was not long till the bus came, and Trixie deposited her companion near the proper flight gate in the *Aeronaves* building. "I'm going to stay with you till loading time, but first I'll check again with the information booth in this building, too, just to make certain everything is all right. Stay here. I'll be back in a few minutes. I'll get a cool drink for you, too."

Trixie stood in line impatiently until her turn came at the window. When she had verified her information, she bought an iced Coke at a refreshment counter and hurried back.

The Mexican woman was scribbling busily on a pad of paper. As Trixie approached, she tore off a sheet and thrust it into her pocket. She accepted the refreshing drink. "You a good girl," she told Trixie. "You got a good heart. You take good care of me. I not forget. Good things happen to good girls. I tell fortunes. I know."

"Thank you," Trixie said, embarrassed. "Lots of nice things have already happened to me. My parents wouldn't agree with you that I'm always good, though.

I've never known any fortune-tellers, but thanks for saying something good will happen to me. I believe your plane is ready now. Don't worry anymore. You'll see your daughter real soon."

The woman reached into her red cotton bag and put something quickly into Trixie's hand. "I give you pretty purse for pretty girl. Use right away. Don't wait!" She looked earnestly into Trixie's eyes. "It is more than purse. It is great fortune. *Cuidadito! Vaya usted con Dios!*"

"Why, thank you! It's beautiful! Good-bye!"

Trixie tucked the gay straw purse under her arm and hurried to the bus that would take her back to her friends.

At the TWA building she found Mart striding back and forth impatiently. The Bob-Whites were obviously relieved when they saw her. "We'd have had to go down to meet them without you in another minute!" Mart said. "After the way you worried for fear we wouldn't be here in time to welcome them!"

"Take it easy, Mart. We're shaving it close, but we're in time." Brian, the oldest Belden, was the acknowledged arbiter. "There they are now! Just coming through that door! Hi!"

A tall, dark boy with a crew cut (Ned Schulz), a pretty, black-haired girl (Barbara Hubbell), and a boy who looked amazingly like her (her twin, Bob) came down the corridor, smiling and waving. The girls hugged Barbara, and the boys all shook hands.

"We hated it when the plane was late—hated to

miss even one hour in New York!" Barbara was breath-less. "I guess we collect our baggage upstairs, don't we?"

"Yes, and we'll get the bus there," Trixie said.

"Gosh, it's great to have you here!" Jim said heartily.

Bob grinned. "Barbara's had her bag packed for a week!"

Ned followed quickly after Brian and Mart. "Boy, look at the crowd! It makes me dizzy. But I like it! I adapt quickly. Say, Trixie, the gang at Rivervale High is still talking about those long shots you made on the basketball court."

"I've never been able to do it since," Trixie admitted. "I guess I'm just a ham. I work better with applause. Here is where we get your luggage."

They stood around a huge turntable, watched their baggage pop up, claimed it, and went out laughing. They crowded into seats in back of the smiling bus driver.

All the way into the city they chattered happily. The driver put his hand over his ear in mock protest, but they laughed him down. "I have a couple just like you at home," he said. "Here we are at East Side Terminal. Everybody out!"

Two cabs took them from the terminal to the apart-ment house on Central Park West. The elevator whisked them to the penthouse, where Miss Trask, tall, gray-haired, smiling, opened the door to welcome them. Then they separated. The boys went across the hall to the other apartment and the girls to the pretty bedrooms in the Wheeler apartment.

Later, when they had freshened up, they met in the Wheeler living room. Miss Trask had disappeared to another part of the apartment. "She's a wonderful person," Trixie told the visitors. "The very best chaperon in all the world."

"You said it!" Jim agreed. "She works overtime at keeping out of sight, and the truth is she's *never* in our way. She likes us and we like her. She's never yet disapproved of anything Honey or I have done."

"She used to be my math teacher at boarding school," Honey explained. "Now she keeps house for us, and we couldn't love her more if she were a relative. She said her sister is getting better but still has to stay in the hospital quite a while to recuperate. She had an operation. Miss Trask stays there every day and comes back here to be with us at night. She's been almost as excited as we've been over your visit."

"She seems super!" Bob said.

"After all you told us about her and how good all the people around the Manor House have been to you Bob-Whites, we sure are glad to meet her now," Barbara said.

"If she'd been around out at Kennedy International Airport, we wouldn't have come so near missing you," Mart said. "She calls our intrepid sister 'Unpredictable Trixie.' Say, Trix, you never did tell us anything about your odd friend at the airport."

"She hasn't had a chance," Honey said quickly, then explained to the visitors about the elderly stranger Trixie had befriended. "I know she made her plane all right, but what was her trouble, Trixie? Who was she?"

Trixie told them of the poor woman's predicament and showed them the bright straw purse.

"It's perfectly perfect!" Barbara looked admiringly at her friend. "Trixie, you're always doing nice things for people."

"And collecting loot." Mart grinned. "Trix, why didn't you tell her to fill the purse with gold?"

Trixie didn't answer. Her face was thoughtful.

"Hey, come out of it," Mart said. "I was just joking. Barbara's right. You always *are* helping people. It gets you in trouble, too, sometimes. Say, what's the matter? Has the cat got your tongue?"

Trixie shook her head vigorously, smiling a broad smile. "I guess I did go off into outer space. I'm sorry. There was something very mysterious about that woman, though . . . the way she looked at me when she left. I wonder!"

"Oh, Trixie, not again!" Mart wailed. "No detective work while we're in the city."

"The things that happen to Trixie are the most . . . the utter most!" Barbara said, so excited her voice ended in a thin squeak. "Our sheriff said she worked on that sheep-thief mystery at Happy Valley like a real professional. Now we may get in on *another* mystery! Trixie, you should write your autobiography right away. I think they'd even make a movie of all your adventures!"

Good-Luck Piece · 2

DON'T YOU THINK it would be a good idea to forget about the Mexican woman now?" Miss Trask suggested. She had brought in tall glasses of lemonade for the Bob-Whites and their guests from Iowa and had overheard part of the conversation about Trixie's experience at the airport. "You helped someone, and she rewarded you in the only way she knew—with a gift made in her own country. That doesn't sound like much of a mystery. Why not think about what you want to do this evening instead?"

"It's one thing to tell Trixie to forget about it and another thing to have her do it," Mart said. "Miss Trask, you know very well Trixie will think more about it."

"Of course I will," Trixie said vehemently. "You didn't see the way she looked at me when she left . . . when she gave me the present. It was a queer, deep look. That woman was mysterious, and you all know it. Look at Brian and Jim right now, over in the corner whispering."

Jim's eyes twinkled. "We were talking over what we want to do this evening. I guess we'd better start our real sight-seeing in the morning. What do you want to do most of all?" he asked the visitors.

"Starting tomorrow morning?" Ned asked.

"Yes. Let's begin with Barbara."

"I'd rather leave it up to the Bob-Whites. After all, they practically *live* in New York."

"That suits me," Ned agreed. "How about you, Bob?"

"It's okay, provided we go to the United Nations, the Empire State Building, Rockefeller Center, Museum of Natural History, Central Park, Statue of Liberty. . . ."

Barbara laughed. "Is that what you call leaving it up to the Bob-Whites?"

"We'll do our best to work most of it in," Brian said. "Now, how about tonight? Any suggestions, Miss Trask?"

"Perhaps you can have a nice dinner someplace, then maybe go to an early movie. I must go and get some things ready to take to my sister. Why don't you think about it for a few minutes? I'll be right back," Miss Trask said, leaving the room.

"Did you hear that?" Bob asked. "Isn't she even going to chaperon us at the movie?"

"Of course not!" Trixie said positively. "There are movies not too far from here. Anyway, Miss Trask is no snoop. She trusts every one of us. She always tells the boys—and she'll tell you and Ned, too—to look after us and feel responsible for us."

"I'd be willing to do that as far as Honey and Di are concerned," Bob said, laughing, "but gosh, Trixie, being responsible for you would be a big job."

Miss Trask came back into the room. "It's after four o'clock. Why don't you unpack, maybe change your clothes if you wish, then decide where to dine?"

"That would be the Automat for me!" Bob said.

Mart exploded. "Not with my appetite! We'd end up with a piece of pie out of a slot in the wall and a glass of milk or a cup of coffee. Don't you want more than that?"

"He probably does," Trixie said. "If you want to go to the Automat, Bob, we'll go there for breakfast sometime. There's one in Times Square. If we're going to the movie tonight, though, I think it'll be a good idea to find a restaurant that's nearer. What movie would you like to see? If you name it, it's sure to be playing someplace in Manhattan."

"How wonderfully wonderful!" Barbara exclaimed. "May we just watch the theaters as we walk along, then decide which movie?"

Trixie turned to the others. "Will that be all right?" When they nodded their heads, she asked Honey,

"Don't you think they'd like to go to that French restaurant on Fifty-seventh Street for dinner?"

"We can try it," Honey answered.

Trixie and Honey already had unpacked their own bags, so they waited in the living room while Diana went to Barbara's room with her.

"It didn't take me long to unpack," Trixie said. "I didn't bring many clothes with me. Did you?"

"No, but if I were as beautiful as Di, I'd want lots of clothes."

"You are, too, Honey, every bit as pretty. Di brought two suitcases with her. It'll take her a while to unpack."

"Yes, it will. And—about being beautiful—you don't realize how pretty you're getting to be, Trixie Belden. Let's take a walk. I'm so jumpy. My insides are like Fourth of July sparklers. I suppose part of it is because I'm so glad the twins and Ned are here."

"Oh, let's *do* walk. I can't possibly sit still. I have the queerest feeling that we're just at the beginning of the biggest adventure yet!"

The girls walked south along Central Park West, then turned on one of the side streets to go around the block.

"When you talk about the 'biggest adventure yet,' the sparklers inside of me turn to ice. I'm shivering. We've had some pretty scary things happen, Trixie. I don't want the twins and Ned to have anything unpleasant spoil their visit. Wasn't Bob cute about the Automat?"

"A lot of people think of New York City as being

27

full of Automats, taxicabs, high buildings, and gangsters. Say, Honey, look at this odd little shop!"

Trixie paused in front of the window of a small antique store. Through the glass they could see a motley collection of articles: vases, lamp bases, old guns, antique jewelry.

The girls put their hands to their eyes and peered into the room back of the window display.

"There isn't a thing in there as nice as the antiques we had in our show at Sleepyside," Trixie said. "Did you ever see such a conglomeration as this?"

"I've never seen anything like that queer little statue over on the left side. Do you see it? It's carved wood. Isn't it odd?"

"That's right. It's so ugly it's darling! Let's go inside so I can see it better."

"You aren't actually thinking of buying it, are you?" Honey asked in surprise.

"I don't know till I find out what it costs and, at least, not till I see it closer. It sort of sends me."

Inside the shop Honey whispered, "It's scary in here. The light's so dim. Here comes the owner."

At Trixie's request the man, swarthy and dark, took the small image from the window. Trixie held it in her hands, turned it over, and examined its rough brown surface. "What is it supposed to be?"

"Some kind of an Incan idol, I guess," the man said. "I don't really know what this one is. My friend who owns this place gets lots of queer stuff from South America. I'm just staying in the shop for him for an hour or two. He'll be back after a while, if you want to come back again. A man left this idol for him shortly after he left, and I just stuck it in the window."

Trixie stood the small statue in the palm of her hand, amused at its grotesque expression. "I just *have* to have it," she announced to Honey. "How much is it?" she asked the man.

"I don't know," the man answered. "Nothing in here has a price tag on it. My friend told me he gets what he can for his things. What do you think it's worth?"

"You're the one to say."

He named a figure. Then, as Trixie gasped, he came down a little, then a little more, till finally she paid the price and tucked the idol into her purse.

"Heavens, that's about the last thing in the world I'd want to spend any money for," Honey said.

"I don't care. I love it. Moms gave me some money to buy something I'd like while we're in the city, and this is it. I'd rather have it than a new sweater."

"Imagine that! What will you do with it?"

"Carry it in my purse for a good-luck piece." Trixie stopped short where she stood. "That reminds me. That Mexican woman told me to use the purse she gave me immediately. She was deadly serious about it. I wonder why."

"Everyone likes to think a gift will be used. That's all there was to it, probably. Jeepers, Trixie, look at the time!"

The girls hurried back to the apartment. Even then, Mart exploded when they got off the elevator. "For pete's sake, Trixie, where have you been? We were just about ready to call the police."

Trixie, mumbling an apology, went past Mart into the apartment. "I suppose Miss Trask is upset with me."

"She had to go to the hospital. She left right after you did. It's a good thing you told her, at least, you were going for a walk. And some walk! Did you go down to Battery Park?"

"Now, Mart, you're the only one who's excited." Barbara smiled. "I wasn't worried. I just finished unpacking and changing my dress. I'm so excited about being in New York!" Barbara's eyes were starry.

"Just look at what I found in the oddest little shop. That's what took us so long. Look at this!" Trixie held the statue for all of them to see. "Isn't he adorable?"

"What in the world is it?" Mart asked.

"Huh-uh . . . don't touch! Just look. The man called it some kind of an Incan idol."

"I think it put a spell on Trixie," Honey said. "Did you ever see anything quite like it?"

"It *is* a queer one," Jim agreed. "I'm not surprised it caught Trixie's eye."

"Her pocketbook, you mean," Brian said. "What did it set you back, Trix?"

"It was my own money, and I'll keep the price a secret. You do, too, Honey!" she cautioned and returned the idol to her purse.

"I don't care what it cost. In fact, I find myself

curiously nonchalant about the whole fugacious performance," Mart said smugly.

"But not aphonic . . . rather ebullient," Bob said glibly and grinned mischievously.

"Whoops! He beat you at your own game!" Trixie exclaimed.

Mart held up his two hands. "I surrender!"

Given a choice of several restaurants, the Iowans selected a French one near the theater district.

"Because I can't *wait* to see Broadway," Barbara said.

"Because it's near Times Square," Ned said.

"Because I'll finally be able to see all those animated billboards," Bob said.

A haze of light from the late afternoon sun filtered through the trees as the young people rounded Central Park and approached Lincoln Center. Children no longer played in the park. Men and women hurried along the sidewalks, pushing one another in their haste and calling out quick apologies.

"Everybody hurries here," Ned said. "Gosh, how can they, when there's so much to see?" His eyes were wide and shining. His own steps quickened to the tempo of those around him. Barbara, flanked by Brian and Mart, was speechless as a galaxy of neon lights came into view and the bustle and noise of the great city closed around them.

"One of those places is where we'll go to the movie after dinner," Jim said. "Dan, stay on the other side of Trixie, and, Bob, keep your eye on Di. Where's Honey?"

"Right here behind you. I'm trying to keep up with Ned."

"Gosh, I'm sorry," Ned said and took Honey's arm. "I'm sort of dizzy with all the lights. There seem to be millions of places to eat. Which one is ours?"

"Up these stairs," Jim answered and led the way.

They went into a darkened world. Candles flickered on rough wood tables. Across the room a huge fireplace burned real logs. There was a fragrance of roasting meat and tangy salad dressings. From an alcove came the muted sound of strings.

When they had been seated, Jim explained, "If we were a little later, the trio would be playing dance music and we could dance."

Ned raised his eyes from the huge menu. "Where?"

Jim pointed to a small cleared space in the center of the room. "Right there," he said.

"That?" Bob asked. "I thought it was a worn place in the carpet. There'd never be room to move around. Who wants to dance, anyway?"

"I guess just about everyone does, except you," Barbara said.

"We'll certainly go dancing at least *one* evening while you're here; maybe in the afternoon, if you'd rather," Trixie said.

Bob smiled. "You can drop me off at that shooting gallery we passed whenever you go dancing. I can dance in the gym at school anytime, but in New York—boy!"

"Honey, is this a nightclub?" Barbara asked. "I've

seen some of them in movies and on TV."

The Bob-Whites all laughed. Then, when Barbara looked embarrassed, Honey explained, "No, it isn't, Barb. I've never been to a nightclub. Jim and I come to this restaurant often with our parents when we stay for the weekend in our apartment."

"A nightclub serves liquor," Jim said. "It isn't served here. The Frenchman and his wife who own this call it a 'family restaurant.' Mme Geronne supervises all the cooking."

Mart still scanned the menu, his eyes wrinkled in a frown. "It's a good thing you've been taking so much French, Honey. The only thing I see here that I recognize is *oeufs*. How do I get a hamburger?"

"In a French restaurant? A hamburger?" Barbara gasped.

"I *always* order a hamburger, wherever I go," Mart insisted.

"Do you want me to order for you?" Honey asked, looking around the table.

"Oh, yes, please . . . a different dish for each one!" Barbara begged.

"Yeah," Bob seconded. "If I point to one of these things, it's sure to turn out to be eggplant or cauliflower, and I hate both of them."

Honey translated the menu, then gave the order to an amused *garçon*.

"I wish I'd ordered snails!" Bob sighed.

"Boy! Be glad you didn't," Mart told him. "One time when I was here with Jim and Honey and their parents, I saw that fancy item *escargots* and ordered some. Ugh! Gosh! Phooey!"

When they went down into the street after dinner, a fairyland spread around them. Whizzing cars threw their lights ahead in a golden blur. Red, blue, and green neon glowed to outline the names of theaters, restaurants, and even little tobacco and candy shops.

A block or so away, a long line waited at the entrance to a movie theater. The young people took their places, laughing and talking, and before they knew it, they found themselves in the lobby. They found seats just as the feature began. For the next two hours they sat quietly, completely absorbed in the picture.

"You could call this whole thing 'Evening in Paris,'" Ned said as they went out into the street again. "First the French restaurant, then a movie about Paris. That old deaf-mute in Montmartre almost had me weeping. Look at your eyes, Trixie!"

"I just couldn't help it; it was so sad." Trixie sighed heavily. "Shall we walk back or take a taxi?"

"Walk!" they cried in one voice.

"But around Central Park, not through it. Stick close together!" Dan warned. "It's dangerous at night!"

A different crowd filled the streets. Instead of rushing, the people now strolled leisurely. The girls walked slowly, watching beautifully dressed women cross to canopied entrances. They sighed ecstatically as they caught whiffs of imported perfumes. Bob and Ned looked closely at the Rolls-Royce, Mercedes-Benz, and Cadillac cars.

Reluctantly the group walked on, approaching the side street of small shops.

"This is where I found my little statue," Trixie announced. "You can't see a thing in there now. Just a dim light way in the back."

The young people pressed their noses against the window. "I can't see a thing in here except a bunch of old junk. You must have picked the only thing anyone would want to carry away when you chose that Incan idol," Mart said.

"Some queer things find their way to New York City from South America," Jim said. "In spite of the fact that it's so near, I don't think we know much about their people. Say. . . ." Jim's voice dropped to a whisper. "Get a load of those characters at the next window . . . the little guy with the scar!"

Brian looked. "On the move!" he ordered. "Quick! Close in around the girls, fellas. March!"

They walked quickly up the street. There were fewer people now and fewer lights. For some reason she couldn't define, Trixie's heart beat faster.

"I'm scared!" Diana said in a low voice. "Let's hurry faster. It's a good thing we're so near our apartment. Those two men were listening—trying to hear what we were saying. Didn't you notice that when we left they moved over to the window of that antique store? Look back of you, Jim, way back there. They're following us. Hurry!"

"Don't worry, Di; we're home!" Jim herded everyone into the lobby. Then he inserted his key in the door that opened into the elevator entrance to the apartments.

Safe inside, Trixie shaded her eyes and looked out at the street. Then she beckoned to Honey and Jim. "See those men slinking off up the street?" Her voice trembled with excitement. "They're the ones who were following us. I wonder why."

The Paper Prophecy • 3

Now, WHAT DO you think of that?" Trixie said as they stood in the living room. "Does anyone believe me now when I say something mysterious is going on?"

"I do!" Barbara said quickly. "Isn't it exciting?"

"I don't." Mart went to the window, pulled back the curtain, and looked down at the street below. "Dan has everyone all worked up with his stories about wicked New York."

"I didn't tell you half of it," Dan said defensively. "There may not be a mystery now—I don't think there is—but those men definitely followed us. They're probably a couple of cheap thieves."

"It's a cinch they don't have anything to do with the Mexican woman at the airport, anyway," Mart insisted.

"That's when Trixie began to act mysterious."

"I never underestimate any idea Trixie has," Jim said. "If you remember some of the things that have happened to us, you won't, either, Mart."

Trixie smiled at Jim. "Thanks. There's a chance I may be wrong about the whole thing. I just have one of those queer feelings in my bones."

"Everybody watch out, then!" Mart warned, a twinkle in his eye.

"Boy, I hope she's right!" Bob's eyes shone.

Brian yawned ostentatiously. "At midnight I don't care too much whether she's right or not. Is anyone sleepy besides me?"

"I think we all are." Jim opened the door that led to the hall and to the boys' apartment. "Everyone up early in the morning! We've lots to do. Come on, fellas!"

Miss Trask had gone to her room as soon as they got home. Honey and Trixie said good night to Barbara and Diana at the door to their room. Honey went ahead of Trixie to turn on the light on the nightstand in the room they shared.

"I'm as wide-awake as an owl," Trixie said thoughtfully as she curled up in a comfortable chair. "How about you?"

"I'm not sleepy, either, for some reason," Honey answered.

"It's been quite a day. I wonder if that Mexican woman found her daughter waiting for her when the plane reached Mexico City."

38

"She seems to be on your mind all the time, Trixie. Why?"

"I don't know. It was good of her to give me this pretty handbag, wasn't it?" Trixie picked up the straw bag, stretched the top to open it, and looked inside.

"There's a coin purse in it. I wish it could be filled with gold, as Mart said when he was teasing me. Think what I could do for Moms if that ever happened! Why, Honey, there's a folded paper here. I wonder what it says."

Trixie unfolded the note excitedly and spread it on her lap. "There's writing on it in some strange language. Look at it, Honey. What language is it?"

"Spanish, I think. Do you suppose the woman wrote you a letter?"

"Could be," Trixie said thoughtfully. "She was busy writing something when I brought the drink to her. It isn't a letter, though. It's funny. It's a sort of verse. What can it be? Do you know any Spanish, Honey?"

"Very little. I can recognize a word here and there. There's *grande*. It means 'big.' "

"Or 'great,' maybe."

"Yes. Then here's the word *cabezo*. Do you know that one?"

" 'Head.' *Grande cabezo* . . . 'big head.' Someone's big-headed."

"She couldn't possibly have meant that you were big-headed, Trixie," Honey declared loyally.

"She'd never have said it to me even if she thought it. Anyway, there's the word *hombre* . . . 'man.' It must mean 'big-headed man.' Honey, when she gave me the purse I remember she said the word *cuidadito*."

"Heavens, that means 'beware'!"

"I don't understand that at all. Just before she went out to her plane, she said to me, 'It is more than purse. It is great fortune.' I surely wouldn't beware of great fortune. I'd run toward it."

"Then why are there words on this paper like *lamento*? It means 'cry.' And *ladrones*, which means 'thieves'?" Honey looked at the paper more closely. "Here's *riesgo*, which surely means 'danger.'"

"*Pistolas*, too, Honey. That means 'guns,' doesn't it? Here's the word *villano*, too. I don't even need to know Spanish to be sure that means 'villain.'"

"You're right. Trixie, I know now why my mother and father are always telling me I should know one foreign language fairly well."

"That's because you'll probably go to Europe with them soon. You know French. Just think how you ordered for all of us in that French restaurant."

"Oh, that! Anyone could do that. Just look at me now . . . an exciting piece of paper in front of us, and I can't get any sense out of it at all because I don't know the Spanish language. Say, wait a minute . . . Miss Trask speaks Spanish almost as well as she does English."

"I know that. What good will it do us right now, though, to know that Miss Trask can figure out what this paper is all about? She's sound asleep. It's one o'clock . . . a million hours till morning, when we can ask her what that Mexican woman meant."

Honey folded the paper and replaced it in Trixie's straw purse. "Right there it's going to stay until morning, when Miss Trask can help us with it. Let's go to bed, Trixie."

"I can't stand to go to bed. I don't think you can, either, Honey Wheeler, even if you do act so calm. Have we ever in our lives had anything like this happen to us? Have we?" Trixie's voice rose in excitement as she spoke.

"No, we haven't," Honey admitted. "It's the middle of the night, though, Trixie. Don't you understand? You never could wait for anything."

Trixie smiled. "Maybe I don't have to wait for this, either. Did you hear Miss Trask's door open?"

Honey didn't have time to answer before a light knock sounded on their door. "Come in, Miss Trask!" she invited.

"I heard your voices. You sounded upset about something. What can it be to have kept you awake so long?" Miss Trask closed the door silently and approached the girls.

"It's this." Trixie showed her the paper.

"Hmmm . . . sort of odd couplets, aren't they? Where did you get this piece of paper?"

"It was in that straw handbag the Mexican woman gave me. It's very important, I know. She told me the purse would mean a fortune. Jeepers, Miss Trask, if you can make any sense out of this, tell me quickly or I'll die!"

"Calm down, Trixie. You're so dramatic." Miss Trask smiled at Trixie's enthusiasm.

Honey sat down on the bed next to the older woman. "Do translate it, if you can," she begged. "There are words in it that frighten us."

"Maybe they *are* frightening words, but I know, somehow, the Mexican woman meant good fortune for me," Trixie added.

Miss Trask glanced again at the paper, then started to speak.

"Please, darling Miss Trask, don't ask us to wait till morning," Honey begged. "If you do, you can just figure on putting Trixie in the hospital at sunrise. She'll never be able to bear it. I won't, either."

"Now who is being as dramatic as Trixie?" Miss Trask inquired. "Just sit quietly, both of you, for about fifteen minutes, and I'll see what I can do. I'm so wide-awake I can't sleep. I might as well try to do what you want me to do."

"Isn't she marvelous?" Honey whispered under her breath.

"Heavenly!" Trixie agreed.

They both sat without making a sound, without even moving a muscle, while Miss Trask found a pencil and paper on their bedroom desk. She read. Then she wrote. She wrinkled her forehead, puzzled. She wrote again, hastily and easily for a while. Then she sat, puzzled, turned the paper over, and scribbled some more. Half an hour passed. The girls still waited without speaking.

"Does this make any sense at all to you?" Miss Trask finally asked, and read:

"Great-headed man, with blinking eye,
A shaded road, a horse's cry,
Foreign words for all to hear,
First clue is now so very near.
Watch out for thieves; they're everywhere,
At home, on island, dead beasts' lair.
Where shines a beacon 'cross the sky,
Beware, great danger lurks close by.
Be not misled by evening's fun;
A villain's work is never done.
When guitars play, thieves linger 'round,
But not till later are they found.
Twin rails of steel, a trembling square,
Watch close, you'll see the guilty pair.
A lonesome journey, gleaming gun,
Foolish girl, what have you done?
Great-headed man does prostrate lie,
A bright stone in his blinking eye.
All is not lost, though, little friend;
Rejoice, for peril, danger end
Near silver wings, past river's bend.
Fortune is yours, fit for a king,
And hearts of little children sing."

"Jeepers, what on earth could all that mean?" Trixie asked, awed.

"It doesn't mean a single thing to me," Honey said forthrightly. "I never heard of such a meaningless, mixed-up lot of words in my whole life. I don't think that paper was ever meant for you, Trixie. I doubt

43

if the Mexican woman even knew it was in the hand-bag she gave you."

"Yes, she did, Honey," Trixie said positively. "Look at what it says at the top of the paper, Miss Trask."

"Hmmm, yes. It does say 'Trixie, *cuidadito!* The woman meant it for you, all right, Trixie. It's interesting, isn't it? That woman was no common fortune-teller."

"That's what I tried to tell all of you."

"You're right, Trixie," Honey said. "I wouldn't be surprised to learn now that she's a seer and kings and queens consult her before they ever make a move!"

Miss Trask laughed heartily. "I'd not go that far. That sort of thing happened way back in the time of King Louis XVI of France. This paper is just a little jabberwocky the Mexican woman amused herself with while Trixie was busy at the information desk. It doesn't mean a thing. If fortune-tellers were ever to foretell anything, don't you think the President of the United States would have one on his cabinet?"

"I guess it was a little silly," Honey admitted slowly.

Trixie didn't admit any such thing. She just said casually, "Thanks so much for translating the note for me. It was thoughtless of me to ask you to do it in the middle of the night. I'll put it back in the hand-bag right away."

When Miss Trask had gone back to her room, how-ever, and Trixie and Honey had climbed into their beds, Trixie turned on her side before she put out the bed lamp. "That prophecy *isn't* all foolishness, Honey, and you know it as well as I do. I'm going to go over it tomorrow and try to find out what it's trying to tell me."

A sleepy mumble came from Honey's bed. "I'll bet a cookie Mart will make fun of the whole thing."

"He won't have a chance to do it," Trixie declared fiercely. "I'm not going to tell one soul about it, and don't you tell anyone, either—unless, maybe—well, if we have to, we can tell Jim."

"You'll end up by telling all the Bob-Whites. I know you, Trixie."

The next morning Trixie and Honey yawned their way through a delicious breakfast Diana and Barbara had prepared while Miss Trask got ready to go to the hospital.

"You're the last ones in, and you have to wash the dishes," Mart said. "Boy, do you and Honey look like zombies, Trixie! Didn't you sleep well?"

Honey helped herself to bacon from a platter. "Trixie was thinking about those men who followed us. She couldn't figure it out."

"What an imagination! Why would anyone want to hold us up? There were dozens of likelier candidates going by that antique shop every minute. If they wanted to rob someone, they didn't have to come way up here."

"You'll sure make a good flatfoot, Trix," Brian said with a smile. "You don't let a day pass without suspecting someone of something."

"Hold on, there . . . I'm not too sure it was Trixie's imagination working last night," Jim said. "On the other hand, it doesn't seem logical that crooks would be following us. Dad told us to take cabs when we were out at night. That's what we'd better do from now on. What's on the program for today?"

"Anyone for a ride in Central Park?" Ned asked. He got up from the breakfast table and looked down across Central Park West to the park below. "We could get an eyeful of a lot of places around here if we'd take a hansom cab. Besides, I've never ridden *back* of a horse, just *on* one. I had to come from the country to the biggest city in the United States to ride *behind* a horse. That's a switch!"

"I guess what Trixie's father said about New Yorkers never seeing New York must be right," Honey said. "I've never been in a hansom cab in Central Park in all my life!"

"Neither have we—not any of the Beldens," Trixie said quickly. "What about you, Dan?"

Dan laughed. "My budget didn't run to cabs when I lived in the city—unless I could catch a ride on the back end of one."

"You must have had a wonderful life, turned loose in New York," Ned said with obvious envy.

"It wasn't what you might think. An orphan on the streets is not a person for anyone to envy, no matter who he is. Life wasn't too bad when my mother was alive. We were poor, but I don't remember minding that at all. After my mom died, it was difficult until my uncle showed up and took me to Sleepyside. Now I have friends like the Bob-Whites. I don't think I'll ever get over wondering why they let me into their club. . . . I sure did get in with a bad bunch of kids here in the city. I never want to see any of them again. They're down around the Bowery and the waterfront. I never think of them except when someone brings it up, like right now. . . . No, I didn't like being turned loose in New York, Ned. I'll settle for a few strings tied to me."

Everyone was quiet for a while. Then Brian said, "If we're going for a ride in the park, we'd better collect the hansom cabs. Come on, fellas. They'll be down on the Fifty-ninth Street Plaza."

While the boys were gone, the girls washed the breakfast dishes and made the beds. Then Trixie telephoned her mother. Her young brother Bobby, age six, answered.

"Moms is out in the garden watering her flowers," he reported. "Mrs. Wheeler and Di's mother are with her. They came here for coffee this morning. Trixie, did you go to the toy store yet?"

"No, Bobby, I didn't," Trixie replied, smiling to herself. "We'll save that, probably, for someday when you're with us. Will you please call Moms in from the yard so I can talk with her?"

"I will if you say hello to Reddy first. Here he is."

"Arf! Arf!" Bobby's big red setter barked.

Then Trixie's mother answered. Trixie's words tumbled over one another in her haste to tell her mother

47

about the fun they were having in New York.

"Barbara wants to say hello to you," Trixie finished up after a while. "Then Honey wants to talk to her mother, and Di wants to talk to Mrs. Lynch."

The girls were still talking when the boys came back with the cabs. "We have to go now," Trixie said hastily. "The boys have brought the cabs. Moms, I wish you could see them. I'm looking at them right now, down on the street below. The drivers have tall black silk hats. Oh, it's going to be such fun! Goodbye now."

Laughing and chattering, the young people crowded into the cabs, and the Irish drivers touched their whips to the flanks of their horses, turned around, and followed the edge of the park to the Seventy-second Street entrance.

A Treacherous Trip · 4

IN THE PARK the sun was shining, and the morning air was cool. Children played. Mothers strolled with babies in carriages. Pigeons were everywhere, strutting around on their pink feet, making contented *plou plou* sounds in their throats.

The hansom cabs skirted the big lake, which was alive with rowboats carrying families—mothers, fathers, children. Back of the rowboats, children trailed paper boats on strings. One boy had made a flotilla of little aluminum foil boats, and the sun, glinting through the trees, turned them to fairy ships.

It was quiet in the park. The Irish drivers kept up a constant flow of information, and, since the two cabs kept close together, the passengers talked back and forth, exchanging impressions of the park.

One of the drivers, the older one, a round-faced gentleman in his sixties, had been driving a hansom cab for years. "I used to drive for Mrs. Andrew Carnegie," he told his group proudly.

The other driver snorted. "Don't believe a word of it," he said hotly. "He's driven that selfsame cab since Peter Minuit bought Manhattan from the Indians."

"I'm not that big a liar," the old Irishman replied. "But I did drive the old lady herself. She was a great old lady, and she loved the park. She'd always wait for me. She liked everybody. Every year she had red geraniums planted in front of her house up there on Ninety-first Street." He pointed north with the tip of his whip. "It was so working people who rode the buses could see them."

Clop. Clop. Clop. Clop. The patient horses traveled along.

"How big is Central Park?" Barbara asked. "It seems almost as big as the whole city of Des Moines."

"Eight hundred and forty acres," Mart answered quickly.

"That's not much bigger than your Uncle Andrew's farm and ours put together," Ned said.

Bob and Barbara and Ned—in fact, everyone in the two cabs—were fascinated with the park and their two drivers . . . everyone, that is, except Trixie. Her mind seemed miles away.

Honey nudged her. "What's the matter? You look so serious," she whispered.

"I can't help it. I keep thinking about that Mexican woman and what she wrote. Honey, it's coming true!"

"You're fooling. What are you talking about?"

" 'Great-headed man,' " Trixie quoted. "It really means 'big-headed,' as we first thought. If I've ever heard a big-headed man talk, it's that driver with all his boasting."

Honey burst out laughing. Everyone looked at her inquiringly, and she clapped her hand over her mouth. "It's a private joke," she said hastily.

"It sounded funny enough to share," suggested Mart.

"You wouldn't think it funny at all," Trixie said. Then she added to Honey under her breath, "Laugh if you want to, but you'll find out I'm right."

Clop. Clop. Clop. Clop.

"Just look at those boats!" Bob cried. His eyes almost stood out from his head. "Over on that little pond!"

"That's Conservatory Pond," Brian told him. "Do you think we could leave the cabs here, driver, and go over to the pond to look at the boats? I've only been there once before, Bob."

"Let's," Mart said. "The boats are really neat. They're all scale models. Men over there at the Kerbs Memorial Boathouse help boys, and grown-ups, too, to make model boats."

"Gosh!" Bob scrambled out.

Conservatory Pond was a clear mirror set in a green frame of fresh-cut grass. Scale model boats of all kinds and sizes dotted its waters. Their white sails were reflected in the clear water, which rippled gently, stirred by a gentle breeze that sent boats to windward, each with its own self-steering rig.

They all settled themselves on the bank to watch.

"Uncle Andrew gave you a sailboat when we came here before," Trixie said to Brian. "It was becalmed, and you were furious. Do you remember?"

"I was furious because I sat here for hours waiting for it to come to shore." Brian laughed, remembering. "Then I had to leave. I don't know what ever became of it."

"The men at the boathouse over there probably hauled it in and, when no one claimed it, gave it to some boy—maybe like that one over there." Trixie pointed to a boy lying prone on the bank, his eyes never leaving his boat, just launched.

"He makes me think of Stuart Little in E. B. White's book," Honey said. "Remember how he sailed the schooner *Wasp* to beat the big racing sloop?"

"He sailed 'straight and true,'" Trixie quoted, "and sent the sloop yawing all over the water."

"Everyone was so surprised to see a mouse at the helm," Honey said, laughing. "They kept yelling, 'Atta mouse! Atta mouse!'"

"He had a terrible time before he ever made port," Mart remembered. "The water was rough; the wind was blowing up a gale."

"I wish the wind were blowing today," Bob said, looking around him. "We'd see some action with those sails all filled. Gosh, do we have to leave?"

"I'm afraid we do," Trixie told him. "We have miles to go and many, many other things to see."

Reluctantly they went back to the carriages, where they found both cabbies snoozing while the horses chomped at the feed bags.

"I never saw a park so full of statues," Barbara said as the old Irishman sat up and rubbed his eyes. "There's one of Hans Christian Andersen, of the Ugly Duckling, the Mad Hatter, and Alice in Wonderland, and—"

"Statues?" the driver repeated. "Yes, statues. It's a queer thing, though. You'll not see a sign of a statue of William Cullen Bryant, him that thought up the whole idea of Central Park."

"William Cullen Bryant?" Trixie remembered her English class at Sleepyside. "He was a Massachusetts poet."

"He was born there," the Irishman corrected her. "But for fifty years he lived right here in New York. He edited the best newspaper New York ever had, the *Post*. In an editorial, way back in the eighties, he spoke out for a city park where people could breathe clean air. The idea caught on, and all this land was bought piece by piece. It cost a fabulous sum . . . about seven million dollars. Today this very same land is worth over *five hundred million* dollars. A pity they never put up a statue to the greatest poet that ever lived."

"Dad always said if you want any information, ask

a hansom cab driver or the driver of a taxicab," Jim whispered to the others. "Shall we go to the zoo now?"

"Gosh, yes!" Bob said.

"Then, if it's all right with the rest of you, we'll go out of the park at Seventy-ninth Street, down Fifth Avenue, driver, and back into the park at the zoo."

"Right-o, laddie!" the old Irishman said and led off with his carriage.

Trixie sat down in the second cab, next to Mart. She wriggled around, stood up again, looked back at the crowd around the pond, sat down again, then turned her body completely around.

"What's the matter with you?" Mart asked disgustedly. "Don't you think the driver knows where he's going? What *is* the matter?"

"I don't want to tell you. You're always making fun of everything I say."

"Did you think you saw someone you knew back there?" Jim asked in a low voice.

"Yes, Jim," Trixie replied soberly. "Those men we saw at the antique shop window. The ones who followed us last night."

"Where?"

"Over on the bridle path, parallel to this road. Can't you see them? Oh, bother! They're gone now."

The carriages had reached the edge of the park. The driver pulled up his horse and waited for a chance to slip alongside the Fifth Avenue traffic.

Just as he saw his opportunity, just as he turned his horse south, two rough-looking men shot out of the park and caught his horse's reins. The frightened animal reared, whinnying loudly. The abrupt stop almost tumbled the driver from his seat.

Trixie and Jim rose in the carriage to help him, but as Trixie stepped from the cab she was tripped. She stumbled and fell to the pavement. One of the strange men swooped down and tried to pry her purse from her arm. With a quick uppercut Jim sent the man sprawling. Howling with pain, he got to his feet and fled with his companion, just as a mounted policeman rode out from the park.

In a few minutes he had the traffic unsnarled, the bruised driver back in his seat, and everything under control.

"It was those same men!" Trixie said emphatically, rubbing her elbow. "I told you I saw them in the park, Jim. The same ones who followed us last night. They're thieves."

"What were they after?" the policeman asked.

"My purse!" Trixie said indignantly.

"I think not," the old Irish driver said. "Not a little girl's purse. They have grander ideas than that, the rapscallions. They were like as not making a quick getaway from some job. They made off in a great hurry."

"They went into a car that was cruising along the Avenue. I saw them!" Ned said. "They brushed by our carriage and went north."

"The things that happen now in broad daylight!" the policeman said. "Everyone has sense enough to stay out of the park at night. But daylight! Are you all right, miss?"

Trixie couldn't answer. Tears got in the way.

"Your knee is bleeding!" Honey cried, horrified. She used her handkerchief to try to stop the flow. "It's a disgrace! Those men should be put in jail!" Honey looked at the policeman.

"There's little the officer can do," the old Irishman put in. "Sure, they were a couple of crooks runnin' away from a job. We just happened to be in the way. Shall I stop at the drugstore so you can get some Band-Aids?"

The policeman jotted down their names and where they lived, then moved on.

"I think, instead, we'll just go straight back to the apartment," Brian told the driver. "I'll look after your cuts there, Trixie. Some Merthiolate and a bandage will do the trick." Brian planned to be a doctor someday, and he was always eager to do first-aid work. "Does your knee hurt very much?"

"Not too much," Trixie sputtered, "but I'm mad clear through. I've ruined my brand-new pantyhose, and I'm afraid the afternoon is spoiled. I can't go to the zoo looking like this! *Please* go without me, won't you, Ned, Bob, Barbara?"

"I don't want to go anyplace till I'm sure you're not badly hurt, Trixie," Barbara declared firmly. "Heavens, bad things surely can happen in this city, as well as good things."

"That's what I've been trying to tell you, Barbara."

Dan helped her back into the carriage. "You can't wear rose-colored glasses all the time—not in New York!"

"You're dead right, Dan," Jim agreed. "I'm sure Trixie's going to be all right, though. I'll go back to the apartment with her . . . Brian, too. The rest of you go on to the zoo."

"*Please* do," Trixie begged. "All I need is an antiseptic and some fresh stockings."

"I'll go with you," Honey insisted. "The rest of you can tell us about the zoo later."

"It Isn't Any Joke!" • 5

TRIXIE LIMPED SLIGHTLY as they left the cab at their apartment. "It *did* hurt you more than you admitted, didn't it, Trixie?" Brian asked. "Sit down here and let me look at it. Say, the skin sure took a beating. It's all off your knee. I'd better put a bandage on it as soon as I clean it thoroughly."

"Brian, it doesn't hurt at all," Trixie insisted. "Heavens, when you think of all the accidents Bobby has! I can't remember him without a bandage on his body somewhere. The only thing that hurts me is thinking about those terrible men. And they got away! You landed a good punch on that shorter one, Jim. He'll remember that for a while."

"You don't suppose he could possibly have thought

the horse was going to run away, do you, and really was a hero trying to stop him?" Honey's face showed her concern.

"Don't waste any tears over him," Trixie answered. "I saw the two men slinking along trying to hide behind the shrubbery just before we turned onto Fifth Avenue—you know I mentioned it to you, Jim. And furthermore. . . ." Trixie stopped, put her hand over her mouth, and looked quickly at Honey.

"Furthermore, what?" Jim asked. "What were you going to say?"

"Shall I tell him?" Trixie asked Honey.

"You might as well. You've been dying to for hours."

"Tell me what?"

"I'll *show* you."

Trixie opened her straw handbag and found the folded paper. "What do you think of this? The Mexican woman at the airport tucked it into my purse. Honey and I found it last night. It was written in Spanish. Miss Trask translated it for us. What do you think of it?"

Jim read the couplets through hurriedly, then passed the paper on to Brian. He looked puzzled.

"It sounds like something out of *Alice in Wonderland*," he said. "It has just about as much sense as the 'Jabberwocky.' What do you think, Brian?"

"I think it was about time that woman left the country," Brian replied, handing the paper back to Trixie. "They probably put her in a straitjacket when she got to Mexico City."

Trixie limped over to the sofa, sat down, and put her leg up to rest. "You couldn't be more mistaken," she said solemnly. "I was impressed with the prophecy from the very start. Now I'm convinced it isn't any joke. It's real."

"What are you talking about?" Honey asked.

"Just this—if you haven't noticed it. Look at the very first two lines. 'Great-headed man' . . . that's the cab driver who thought he knew it all. 'Shaded road' . . . that's the road through the park. 'A horse's cry' . . . well, that horse whinnied like mad when the man grabbed the reins. What more do you want from a prophecy?" Trixie looked about her triumphantly.

"Trixie Belden, you can read anything into two lines that you want to read!" Brian said impatiently. "Look at all the rest of it. What do you make of all the rest of the crazy things on the paper?"

"I don't know, but I'm sure going to find out," Trixie stated firmly. "Jim, you think there's some sense to it, don't you?"

"I didn't at first. It's beginning to get through to me, though. Say, Trixie . . . it's terrific!"

"I know it," Trixie said happily. "Barbara and Bob and Ned would think so, too, if they knew about it."

"Don't worry." Honey spoke a little sharply. "You'll let them in on it just as you did Jim and Brian, when the right time comes."

Trixie's face fell. Honey ran to her quickly and dropped on her knees beside the sofa. "Oh, Trixie, I wasn't criticizing you. I think you *should* tell the others. It'll be heaps of fun to watch what happens from now on."

"The trouble with the darned thing," Brian mused, "is that we can't figure out what it means till after it's happened."

"That's right. I don't like all the 'guns' and 'dangers' and 'bewares' that run through the thing." Jim shook his head as though he'd like to clear his brain. "What's the matter with me, anyway? You'd think I really believed in it!"

"I'll have to wait till more of it unrolls before I commit myself." Brian walked to the window and looked out. "The rest of the gang is back from the zoo. The cab's just stopping down in front to let them out. Tell them, Trixie, and see what they think."

Barbara and Bob, Ned, Diana, Dan, and Mart burst through the door of the apartment, all talking and laughing at once.

"Gosh, the zoo was the greatest!" Bob said happily. "How are you feeling, Trixie?" He looked at Trixie with concern. "What did her knee look like, Brian?"

Barbara slipped off her shoes and curled up in a chair. "You look a lot better, Trixie," she said, "but kind of queer. You look funny—odd. . . ."

"Yeah, what's up?" Mart asked curiously. "Come on, give!"

So Trixie and Honey, talking together, told them about the prophecy and let them read it. Jim called their attention to its application to the incident outside the park that morning.

Excited, they sat on the floor in a circle, shouting out as each couplet was read. Mart ridiculed it from time to time, although he didn't miss a word that was read.

Miss Trask arrived to find them sitting, sprawling, and pacing the floor. Barbara was hopping from one stockinged foot to the other.

"What happened?" Miss Trask asked quickly when she spied the bandage on Trixie's knee.

"I'm all right!" Trixie said reassuringly. "But listen to what really happened!"

After they told her, Miss Trask said sadly, "I wish I'd never translated it for you." Her voice quieted them. "I can see what is going to happen from now on. Trixie Belden, you'll actually *wish* those awful things into happening."

"I honestly won't do any such thing," Trixie said, laughing. "I'm not silly enough to think anyone would know in advance what is going to happen to anyone. It's just fun and exciting."

Miss Trask sighed, appearing somewhat relieved. "I don't know what to think about you, Trixie. I really can't decide."

"You're not alone in that, for sure," Mart said fervently.

"I *like* Trixie," Barbara said indignantly. "I think it's the most wonderful, wonderful thing in the world to be near her. Things happen!"

"You can say that again," Mart admitted. "When do we eat around here? I don't suppose Trixie had better go out anyplace tonight."

"We don't want to go anyplace, anyway," Bob and Barbara said, practically in unison. "There are some good programs on TV," Barbara added.

"I've a big casserole ready to pop into the oven," Miss Trask said with a smile. "Trixie should have all the rest she can possibly get if you are all going to see the United Nations tomorrow."

"I'm ashamed of myself. I slept just like a log last night," Trixie said next morning when the group had gathered for breakfast.

"I did, too," Barbara echoed. "I never thought either one of us would shut an eye after all that excitement yesterday. Trixie, you aren't even limping this morning."

"No. I'm good as new. Let's get going. I suppose it's the hospital again for you, Miss Trask?"

"Yes," Miss Trask replied. "I'm quite encouraged about my sister. I'm reading to her now. We both enjoy that. Are you all ready to start? Then let's go down in the elevator together."

Trixie showed very little sign of her injury of the day before as they all walked briskly toward the United Nations buildings.

"My mom and Bob and Barbara's mom have both done a lot of work for UNICEF," Ned said, stepping along at Trixie's side.

"I know," Trixie said with a warm smile. "Barbara rounded up all the children in the neighborhood to collect money for UNICEF on Halloween, didn't she? One of the girls at Rivervale High, when I was visiting in Iowa, told me that the little 'Trick-or-Treaters' raised nearly two hundred dollars."

"That was swell!" Mart said. "I'm going to try to do some organizing myself at Sleepyside this year. I'll see if some of the bigger kids won't lay off the trick stuff and maybe have a special basketball game to raise money for the International Children's Fund instead."

"Say, that's a neat idea," Ned said eagerly. "We can try it at Rivervale, too. Mom and Mrs. Hubbell sell lots of UNICEF Christmas cards every year. Mom wants me to tell her all about the United Nations when I get back home."

"That's a big order!" Brian laughed.

"I don't mean all the things they do here," Ned said hastily. "She just wants me to tell her what the people and buildings look like. My mom and dad belong to a study group, and they really know what goes on at the United Nations."

"We study about it, too, in school," Trixie said quickly. "One of the girls who used to go to Sleepyside High is a guide here—Betsy Tucker. I hope she's on duty when we take the tour."

"I wonder what qualifications are needed to be a United Nations guide," Diana said. "Their uniforms are beautiful!"

"And wouldn't one of them look beautiful on you— that shade of blue, with your violet eyes!" Trixie looked admiringly at her friend. "Do you really think you may want to be a United Nations guide someday?"

"Why not? You and Honey know just what you're going to do when you finish college. By that time your detective agency will be going strong, if you keep on as you've started. I'm going to ask Betsy, when we see her, just what preparation is needed. It isn't too early to think about it."

"You'll have to bone up on languages, that's for sure," Mart said.

"Only French," Honey reminded him. "When we go inside, you'll notice that all signs are in English or French. There are guides from so many countries that almost every language is spoken. Guides from the United States aren't expected to know any language other than French. It's the international language."

"There we are . . . right ahead!" Jim called out. "See the circle of flagstaffs?"

"Wheeew! Is that ever a sight!" Ned stood still, overwhelmed by the nearness of the tall glass Secretariat and the curved line of flags whipped by wind from the East River close by.

Far above the colorful avenue of flags from all member nations rose the standard of the United Nations itself—a white field with an olive wreath.

As they crossed the wide stone plaza that surrounded the entrance to the United Nations buildings, the visitors could see in the distance the great Queensboro Bridge arching above Welfare Island in the East River.

A sight-seeing boat steamed lazily past and tooted its salute.

"We go in here," Brian directed. He held open the door which led to the vast lobby. "There's Betsy waving to us!"

"The Idol Is Worthless!" • 6

A LOVELY GIRL in a blue uniform hurried to greet the Bob-Whites. "How nice to see someone from Sleepyside!"

"You haven't met Dan Mangan," Trixie told her. "He's our newest club member. And these are our friends from Iowa." She presented the Hubbell twins and Ned Schulz. "Do you think you can be our guide?"

"I think so. I'll ask. We take turns, but the tours haven't started yet today and won't for another twenty minutes. In the meantime, wouldn't you all like to meet some of the other guides? Especially some of the ones from other countries?"

"Trixie, this is super!" Barbara cried as Betsy left to find the other guides. "Just imagine what I'll tell my friends at home when I see them!"

"This is Steffi," Betsy said, returning. "She really has a long Hindu name, but she wants us to call her just Steffi."

"How do you do?" Steffi asked in a soft voice. She spoke perfect English. "I have not been here long. I have not met many young people in the United States."

"You *must* have been in our country before," Diana insisted. "You speak English so beautifully."

"I have learned it in our school in Delhi," the girl answered. "All schools in India teach the English language. You are interested in my sari?" She smiled at Honey.

"I didn't realize I was staring so," Honey answered, embarrassed. "It's beautiful!"

"It was woven of blue and silver, the colors of our United Nations. I think you have a lovely sweater . . . and your beautiful brown hair. My hair is so black."

Steffi drew several other girls toward her and introduced them. "This is Arista. Her home was on one of the three large islands near Greece which suffered great damage from an earthquake. One of the agencies of the United Nations International Children's Emergency Fund, UNICEF, helped her relatives after the disaster. Now Arista's family lives in the United States."

"It is my hope to do something for the United Nations in return for what they did for my family,"

Arista said, smiling at the young people.

"It is *my* hope, too," the guide from Morocco said. "It is very inspiring to be here where all nations wish to help one another. In my country almost everyone in our city of Rabat was afflicted with an eye disease that always leads to blindness. Do you know what my father wrote to me a few days ago? He said that for the first time there has been *saif balash ramad.* That means 'summer without eye disease.' Our people in the mountains and on the desert do not know how to read, so it is very difficult to teach them what they must do to prevent eye infection. UNICEF sent motion pictures showing children washing their hands, having their eyes examined, and doctors giving treatment. So much suffering and blindness is being prevented. It's wonderful that my people have had such help."

"In my country, El Salvador," a pretty black-haired girl said, "so many United Nations countries have helped. A public health consultant came from Mexico, a sanitary engineer from Colombia, nurses from the United States. They organized teams to clear my homeland of malaria, going from house to house with spray guns for mosquito control. Malaria has been wiped out!"

"I guess the first thing to be done is to try to make people well," Brian said thoughtfully. "It's a great challenge to doctors. Maybe I'd have a bigger challenge helping with world health projects than I would helping you with your school for boys, Jim."

"Maybe you can do that for a while, then help me

later," Jim said soberly. "I'm sure glad we had this chance to talk to guides from other countries, Betsy. It widens our world, doesn't it? Maybe I, too, could work to better advantage in a larger field."

"Why, Jim, you know very well what you've always said: You have to make small beginnings to accomplish big things," Trixie said loyally. "I think your plan for a school for underprivileged boys is wonderful! Just think," she told the girls around her, "Jim inherited a big fortune from his uncle, and he hasn't touched a penny of it. He's going to invest it all in a school to give boys a chance for education—boys who wouldn't have a chance otherwise."

"That seems a pretty big dream itself!" Betsy said. The other guides clapped, and Jim turned redder than his hair. "It's really what all this whole concept means, isn't it?" Betsy spread her arms to include the dream that was the United Nations. "It's each one helping the other. It's great! Wait till I show you the home of that dream. There's the loudspeaker—listen!"

"Tour number one assembling! Betsy Tucker will be your guide!"

As Betsy led the group to the big area where the plaster models of the buildings had been set up, Trixie touched Barbara on the arm. "Do you mind if I don't go on the tour with you?"

The group halted. "It's your leg. It's hurting you, isn't it?" Barbara asked anxiously. "We shouldn't have tried to come today."

"Oh, no," Trixie assured her hastily, "it isn't that

at all. It's just that every time I come here I go on the tour, and while I learn something new each time, I never get to stay long enough in one place. I'd like to meet you all later, if you don't mind."

"Of course we don't mind." Barbara smiled. "I'm glad that's the reason, rather than a hurting knee."

"I'll stay with you, Trixie," Honey offered. "I'd like to spend some time in the shops. You'll never miss us, you'll be so excited at the things you'll see and hear."

"We'll meet you in the cafeteria when the tour's over," Trixie called after the group as they assembled for the tour.

"Now, Trixie Belden, you can just tell me what that was all about!" Honey exploded when they were a short distance away.

"Calm down, Honey. You *must* know what I want to do. It's as plain as the nose on your face that those men who tripped me yesterday wanted something that was in my purse. I had less than five dollars in money. It wasn't that, was it?"

Honey shook her head, puzzled.

"Well, then, the only other thing I have, aside from my lipstick and dark glasses, is the idol I bought in that antique shop!"

"Why in the world would anyone want that odd little man?"

"That's exactly what I want to find out," Trixie answered emphatically. "There's a shop downstairs where they sell all kinds of things from South America. They're almost sure to have some wood carvings there.

If they don't, whoever is in charge of the booth may know something about my Incan idol. I'll show it to the person in charge."

"Don't show it right away. Find out what you can about the other carvings first, if they have any."

"That's smart of you, Honey. You're right."

The girls went down the steps. There were gay shops on the lower level offering native work from almost every country in the world. Trixie went directly to the South American shops.

All the articles were arranged in small booths. There were handwoven materials, some of them made into bright skirts and jackets; richly colored glass; wrought silver heavily studded with turquoise and other semiprecious stones. There were shaggy wool rugs, crude, highly pigmented paintings and—

"See them! Here they are!" Trixie called, excited. "Carved wooden idols! Honey, they look exactly like my funny little man."

Trixie took Honey's hand, held it tight. They stood on tiptoe to look at a high shelf where a row of small brown idols stood. The idols seemed to have been made from one mold. "Are they wooden, or are they cast in plaster?" Trixie asked the beautiful dark-haired woman in the booth breathlessly.

"They're wooden," she answered. She reached for one and placed it in Trixie's hands.

"It isn't just quite the same, is it, Honey?" Trixie asked, examining the brown object carefully.

"Almost. I think yours is older. Say, Trixie, maybe

that's the answer. Maybe that's what makes those men want to steal it. Maybe it's so old and rare that it's worth a lot of money."

"I have a small Incan idol I bought at an antique store a few days ago," Trixie explained to the clerk. She took it from her purse and passed it over the counter. "Do you know whether or not it is worth anything?"

The woman accepted the statue. She turned it over and over in her hands. "I'm no expert," she said after a moment. "I think they're all frightfully homely. What did you want with one, anyway?"

"I think mine is so ugly it's darling. Then, it isn't an antique?" Trixie was disappointed.

"I told you I'm no expert. There's a man standing right behind you who seems to know a lot about Incan carvings. He was in here about two hours ago and looked over every one I have in stock. Whatever he was looking for, I didn't have it. Mr.—uh—" she called.

"Yes, madame." A short, dark-haired man with deep olive skin answered.

The clerk explained why she had summoned him. When he saw the small statue Trixie drew from her purse, his eyes widened.

"What is it you wish to know?" he asked.

"Why—I—wonder—I just wanted to know if my statue is an antique." The man was beautifully dressed and very important-looking. Trixie imagined he was someone of consequence in his own country.

"May I look at the statue a little closer, please?"

Honey moved up close to Trixie and hissed under her breath, "Hold on to it. Don't let him get his hands on it."

Trixie, completely perplexed, ignored Honey's warning and passed the statue over to the man. He held it to the light, examining every inch of it. Then he looked closely at Trixie and smiled enigmatically. "If someone has sold you this as an antique, miss, I'm afraid you have been victimized. I must not allow that. I shall be glad to take it off your hands for the price you paid for it. Unscrupulous people from my country have been known to bring cheap machine-made work into this country and try to pass it off as handmade."

He took out his wallet. "Whatever you paid, I'll reimburse you."

"I don't want my money back. I want to keep it. I didn't buy it for an antique. I like it just as much even if it isn't." Trixie reached for her statue. The man pushed her hand away and shook his head. "No, miss, I couldn't allow you to have this poor piece of work. If you do not want your money back, I shall replace it with one which is hand-carved. Here is my card. Come to this address tomorrow, and I will give you a better example of the work of my country."

"You are very kind, but I like my own better." Before the man was aware of what was happening, Trixie had retrieved her little idol and put it in her purse.

The man's face flamed. "Are you a crazy girl? The idol is worthless!" He seized Trixie's arm and whirled her around. "You give it back to me!" he demanded.

A crowd, attracted by the man's loud words, gathered. When he realized this, his attitude changed again. He immediately became apologetic. "Forgive me!" he said with seeming abjectness. "I become too excited when I know what bad people in my country are doing. You have made a mistake, miss. I bid you good-bye."

"I don't know what was the matter with him," the clerk at the booth said in amazement. "He got pretty excited when he was here before, looking over my stock. I think he may be a little. . . ." She twirled her finger in a circle in front of her temple.

"Crazy?" Trixie asked.

The woman nodded her head.

"He must be," Trixie agreed. She and Honey turned to go back up the stairs. "Why did you hiss at me like that to warn me?" Trixie asked quickly.

"I didn't trust him from the minute I saw him. Trixie, he wants your statue for some reason or other. Don't ask me why I think so. I don't believe, though, that you've seen the last of him."

"Well, the plot thickens, doesn't it?" Trixie mused. "I must have a pretty valuable little statue on my hands. Everyone said I was silly to buy it, didn't they? Even you said so, Honey."

"You didn't think it was valuable yourself when you bought it. Remember? You just said it was so ugly you wanted it. I have to admit it has turned out to be interesting. Isn't it about time for us to meet

75

the others at the cafeteria?"

"Hardly. I'm tired, though, after that encounter with that man. Honey, he would have knocked me down and taken my statue away from me if there hadn't been a crowd around. There he goes now, down that corridor. Heavens, Honey, his back looks so familiar. Do you possibly think—no—it couldn't be! He's about the same size, though. . . ."

"Are you thinking he's that scar-faced man who tried to knock you down when the horse shied yesterday?"

"I'm thinking that very thing."

"But that man was years older and so shabby. He had another man with him, too. Remember, Trixie? They were both following us home the night before, too. This man doesn't have a scar. I think he may be some wealthy importer. He had an educated way of talking, too."

"Maybe so. It's all peculiar. Let's tell Jim about it when we see him and ask him what he thinks."

"You always say 'ask Jim,'" Honey said mischievously. "Even if he is my brother, I don't think he's all-wise. We'll ask all the Bob-Whites what they think."

Trixie blushed to the roots of her sandy hair. She hadn't any idea that her complete reliance on Jim was so obvious.

"Of course we'll ask all of them. Brian's pretty smart, too. You think so, too, don't you, Honey?"

It was Honey's turn to blush now. "Brian's the

oldest Bob-White," she said, as though that explained everything. "There they are now, both of them, Brian and Jim, and all the rest of the crowd. See them going down the line over there at the cafeteria? Yoo-hoo!"

Brian called back, and Jim waved. Everyone in line smiled as the two girls, faces flushed and eyes dancing, hurried to catch up with their friends.

Break-In • 7

The most exciting thing happened!" Trixie burst out as she put her tray on the table near the others.

"Oh, Trixie, you should have been with *us!*" Barbara's words spilled over one another. "I never saw anything so wonderful in all my life. I hadn't the slightest idea of what the United Nations—"

"I just *have* to tell you first what happened to us—" Trixie hadn't heard a word Barbara had said.

"Barbara's right. Gosh, what we'll have to tell when we go back home! There was this man in the council room at—" Bob almost spilled his glass of milk in his eagerness to talk.

"Wait till I tell you about the man we saw!" Trixie interrupted.

Brian stood up and raised his hand for silence. He was laughing so hard he could hardly talk. "One at a time! No one can tell what either of you is talking about. Trixie will burst a blood vessel if you don't let her tell what she's trying to tell. Is it okay if she speaks first, Barbara?"

Reluctantly, Barbara nodded.

So Trixie told about the sleek-haired man and his interest in her Incan idol, of his insistence that she hand it over to him, and of her determination to hold on to it.

"Trixie has a 'won't' of iron when she makes up her mind," Honey said. "I don't know what might have happened if there hadn't been a crowd of people around us. That man was so oily he was creepy! I wish we could point him out to you."

"Trixie seems to have mixed him up with that little man who was one of the pair who followed us from the antique shop," Mart said. "How do we know she'd ever recognize the man she saw this morning? The guy who tagged us certainly wasn't sleek or well dressed. Forget the whole thing, Trixie, before you get into it beyond your depth!"

"I won't forget it, Mart Belden," Trixie cried. "I won't say anything more about it if you aren't interested, but I won't forget it. Go on, now, and say whatever you have to say, someone, about the United Nations, since nobody seems interested in my story."

"I am!" Barbara cried.

"Gosh, so am I!" Bob said, awed.

"And me, too," Ned added. "Everything happens so fast around here that I never know who to listen to first. Trixie may be entirely right about that man, Mart. He could very well be the same one who followed us. I sure wish we could get a glimpse of him ourselves. We could soon tell if he is the same one."

Ned was destined to have his wish.

Just as the Bob-Whites and their friends were about to get into a waiting cab at the edge of the plaza, Trixie gestured frantically toward a man standing nearby. In the cab, after it had started, she gasped, "That was the man we saw in the gift shop. He listened while you gave the address of our apartment to the cab driver, Jim! Did you see him?"

"*I* saw him, Trix, and I give in," Mart said. "He *is* one of the men we saw at the antique shop. I wonder where his buddy is and what the heck they want with an Incan idol."

"That's something we'll have to find out. I don't like the looks of the whole business," Jim said. "Shall we go back to the apartment now?"

"Maybe it'll be a good thing if we don't," Brian suggested. "If he's following us in another cab, we can throw him off if we don't go right back. He may think he didn't hear the address correctly."

"I guess you all forget that he couldn't have wanted our address at all," Honey said. "If he *is* one of the men who followed us before, he surely knows where we live. He followed us home from the antique shop, didn't he?"

They all laughed, Trixie hardest of all. "You see, Honey, I always told you that you were the smartest member of our firm. That man had some other reason for standing around when we were leaving."

"Counting noses, I guess," Mart said. "There's safety in numbers, you know. He's pretty sure he can't do anything if we all stick together. Moral: All stick together!"

"I think you're right," Trixie said soberly. "He's probably furious after seeing how many of us there are."

"I don't think I can stand it if things keep happening as fast as they have happened!" Barbara exclaimed.

"I can," Ned said quickly. "I love it. Gosh, it's a real mystery, for sure. About the only thing I can do when I get back home is to join the police force and get to work. What are we going to do now?"

"I have an idea," Brian said. "How about us guys going to Lou Tannen's Magic Shop while you girls explore the grocery stores and delicatessens on Fiftieth Street and Second Avenue?"

"That'll be neat!" Mart said. "Then we'll all get dinner together back at the apartment. Is it a deal?" he asked the girls.

"It's a good idea, except for one thing," Honey answered slowly. "We just got through agreeing that we should all stay together from now on."

"Of course!" Brian exclaimed. "Now it's my turn to be a birdbrain."

Jim laughed. "Not you, Brian. Anyway, I don't think

81

we *all* have to stay together *all* the time. How about splitting up into two sections? Dan and I will go with the girls, and you and Mart can go with Ned and Bob to the magic shop. Will that be okay?"

"I don't see why not," Brian replied. "You can put on a magic show for all of us after dinner back in the apartment. See if you can find some of those card tricks you used at my birthday party, Mart."

"I will, if you girls will promise not to come home with just a can of spaghetti and meatballs," Mart agreed.

"He likes kooky foods," Dan explained in mock seriousness, "like gnat's eyebrows. . . ."

"And Brazilian fried ants . . ." Jim added.

"Chocolate-covered . . ." Dan went on.

"Ugh, I won't have any appetite for dinner, I can tell that," Barbara said, rubbing her stomach.

"There *are* chocolate-covered ants in jars at some of those grocers," Dan insisted. "I saw them."

"Grasshoppers, too," Bob said. "Even in a store in Des Moines I saw some canned grasshoppers."

"And preserved grubworms," Jim said. "Yummy!"

"That's enough!" Trixie said. "This is where we part. We'll see you not later than five thirty back at the apartment."

"If you turn out a dinner we can choke down, we may put on the magic show for you," Mart called back. " 'Mart, the Mysterious Manipulator of Magic' —that's me."

"For that, we'll put pink whipped cream on *your*

fried grasshoppers," Barbara said. "We like you, Mart."

"Like this," Mart answered, drawing one finger across his throat.

When Jim and Dan and the girls got back to the apartment, they found Miss Trask, Brian, Mart, Bob, and Ned in excited conversation. Jim unloaded the grocery purchases on the kitchen table. Then they went into the living room to see what all the excitement was about.

"The joint has been cased, pillaged, plundered, spoliated," Mart said out of the side of his mouth.

"Oh, hush, Mart!" Miss Trask said. "This is serious." She repeated what she had been telling the boys. "My sister was sleeping restfully at the hospital, so I decided to come back here. Soon after I returned, a man came to the door and told me he wanted to look at the apartment."

"What did he look like?" Trixie asked quickly.

"Dark, short—I think he was a foreigner," Miss Trask answered. "I asked him who had sent him and why. He said the owner was planning to sublet the apartment."

"Dad and Mother don't want to sublet the apartment, I'm sure," Jim interrupted.

"I'd never heard that they did," Miss Trask went on, "but he said that he was a prospective tenant, that the custodian had told him to come on up to the apartment and he would meet him here."

"I hope you didn't fall for that," Mart said.

"Of course I didn't," Miss Trask said indignantly.

"Did you let him in?" Jim asked quietly.

"No, I told him to wait right there in the corridor while I went to check with the custodian." Miss Trask's voice trembled. "It took me a long time to find Mr. Pebbles. He was working in the building next door. The same company owns both buildings."

"Go on—go on—please!" Trixie begged impatiently.

"He told me he'd be up just as soon as he finished replacing some broken tile on the kitchen floor where he was working. He said he had to finish it while the cement base was still damp—"

"Oh, dear! Miss Trask, what *happened?*" Trixie was almost frantic.

"I'm getting to it, Trixie, as fast as I can. The custodian told me to tell the man to wait in the hall out there."

"Then what?"

"I'll show you what—just follow me!"

She led them to the bedroom Honey and Trixie had been sharing. There wasn't a thing in the room that hadn't been pulled out of place, turned over, or tossed on the floor. Even the pictures were askew; the mattresses had been moved; the bed coverings were wadded into rolls. Dresser drawers lay on their sides, spilling their contents.

"Jeepers!" Trixie said in amazement.

"Thieves!" Honey cried. "I *know* my beautiful watch is gone, the one Daddy gave me for my birthday. Trixie, did you leave your watch here, too?"

"I did. There it is on the dressing table. Your watch is there, too, Honey. It wasn't jewelry he wanted. Here is where one of the men was while his companion was at the United Nations . . . see? What did Mr. Pebbles say when he came up here?"

"He hasn't been here yet; don't you understand?" Miss Trask said. "It just now happened. When I came back to give that man the message from the custodian, he wasn't here. The door to the apartment was open, and I found all this!"

There was a knock at the door.

"That must be Mr. Pebbles now," Jim broke in. "We're here, sir," he called to the custodian.

Mr. Pebbles was puffing. "I thought over what you said, Miss Trask. Then I remembered I hadn't told anyone to look at the apartment. I knew that man was lying and was up to no good. I hurried as fast as I could. He didn't waste any time, did he? Have you checked to see what he got away with?"

Trixie and Honey made a quick survey.

"Not a single thing is missing," they reported after a few minutes.

"I guess he was scared off when he heard the elevator and knew you were coming back, Miss Trask," the custodian said thoughtfully. "How he ever got into the building—I've got it! I had a locksmith working on the entrance door. He must have slipped past him. I'll get the police on the job right away."

A policeman arrived shortly. Bob and Barbara stood wide-eyed while he looked for fingerprints, took down everyone's name, and questioned the Bob-Whites, their visitors, and Miss Trask. Then he left.

"He could have given us some idea of what he was going to do next," Trixie said.

"He's not supposed to talk," Dan told her. "Anyway, what does he know about what happened? Not half as much as you do, Trixie. I can even see your mind working. You think that man was a pal of the sleek gentleman at the United Nations; that both of them are after the Incan idol."

"They could very well be, Dan," Jim said thoughtfully.

"Two smart thugs after one little statue?" Dan was dubious. "I'll believe it when I see it. This guy just saw a chance to sneak past the locksmith and go after the loot. This apartment happened to be first on his list in the building."

"Aren't we going to find out *anything* more now?" Barbara asked, disappointed.

"Not now or ever, or I'll miss my guess," Dan said. "Burglary attempts are made all the time. The police have time to concern themselves only with the jobs where the thieves are successful. Looks like you have a clean-up job here, Trixie."

"Looks to me like Honey and I have work here for our detective agency."

"Looks to me like we'll never get anything to eat," Mart said with a twinkle in his eye. "And you know how I feel about food."

"Yes, you will, too, Mart Belden," Trixie said indignantly. "We've brought all kinds of good things to fix for dinner. We stopped at those stores on Fiftieth Street—"

"And we're all going to pitch in and help," Brian said. He walked into the kitchen and began unloading the individual items from the grocery bag.

"You just sit down and rest, Miss Trask. We'll have everything on the table in a jiffy," Trixie said. "You'll be our guest."

"That will be very nice. I can't sit still, though. I'm too nervous." Then Miss Trask brightened. "I'll straighten up your room."

"You will?" Trixie exclaimed. "You darling, darling Miss Trask! I hate to straighten up anything. I'll make a special portion of beef stroganoff just for you."

Miss Trask's eyebrows went up; then her face relaxed in a smile. "I'll like that, Trixie. Beef stroganoff, indeed!"

Wrong Number • 8

TRIXIE GAVE JIM and Brian lettuce to wash, tomatoes to peel, and green onions to cut up for the salad.

"The only thing I could cook would have so much garlic in it that we'd be run out of the apartment," Dan said with a smile. "Anything I can do, Trixie?"

"You and Ned can run around the corner to that delicatessen and get some Cokes," Trixie said. "We'll want some later in the evening, and there isn't a single bottle here."

"Bring some popcorn, too," Honey added and gave Dan the housekeeping purse. "Maybe some extra butter, too. We *may* want popcorn after dinner."

"You don't have much confidence in my cooking, do you?" Trixie said, laughing. "To be real truthful,

I'm curious to see what I'll turn out myself."

"If you need a chicken sewed up, I can do that," Barbara said.

"I'm pretty good with a needle, too," Honey said, "but just suppose Barbara and I set the table and shine the silver if it needs it."

"I'll help Trixie," Diana said. "I know how to make Chinese fried rice."

"That would be keen!" Mart said. "Now who would like to sample my mashed potatoes *avec fines herbes?*"

"You made that up!" Diana said.

"I did not! I ate potatoes with herbs one time at that French restaurant where we were the other evening. I asked the chef what was in them. I'll bet my potatoes will taste every bit as good as his!"

"Ooo-la-la!" Dan said and pretended to twirl a moustache. "Don't shoot, Mart. I'm on my way."

An hour later the apartment was filled with delicious fragrances. The aroma of crisped beef blended with that of half a dozen herbs and spices. Trixie had flour on her nose, apron, and hands, but she smiled triumphantly. "My beef stroganoff is perfect!" she declared.

"Stop tasting it, then," Mart said, smiling. "There won't be any left."

"Oh, yes, there will be," Trixie sang. "I made the recipe that was supposed to be used for twelve. I just hope you like it. You'll have it again tomorrow."

She was wrong. There wasn't a bit left of the delicious sliced brown beef, smothered in sour cream, spices, onions, and tomatoes. Served with Diana's delicious fried rice, it was perfect. Mart, too, surprised the girls by the way he cooked potatoes to the right fluffiness, put them through a ricer, and produced his French version of mashed potatoes.

"What did you put in them?" Barbara asked as she reached for the dish and helped herself a second time.

"Grated cheese," Mart ticked off on his fingers, "sour cream, nutmeg, mace, thyme, chives, and lemon juice. Then," he added dramatically, "just a taste of sesame seed, dill, and rosemary."

"I never heard of any of those things, except cheese," Dan said, "but the *tout ensemble—c'est parfait!*"

"Jeepers, Dan!" Trixie said, her blue eyes wide. "Where did you learn all that French?"

"Hanging around Greenwich Village," Dan said. "No, honest, Miss Trask coached me before dinner. I was going to throw it in if the girls came up with a bomb. They didn't, though, and the dinner was perfect. So I can say it and mean it. That meat stuff—beef stroganoff you call it, Trix?—that was something!"

"Did you like the *salade,* Monsieur Mangan?" Jim inquired.

"*Mais oui!*" Dan answered. "Well, that's the extent of my French. I think the whole spread was from outer space."

"You can say that again!" Miss Trask said.

"Miss Trask, Miss Trask!" Mart feigned shock. "Watch your language."

"I'll have to watch my weight if Trixie cooks dinner

very often." The Wheelers' housekeeper smiled at the young people.

"If I could only forget for a little while what happened today," Trixie said and winced, remembering. "That man at the United Nations and the burglar here! Oh, well." She shrugged her shoulders. "Who'll wash the dishes?"

The hush was complete.

"All right, then, you'll be drafted!" Trixie announced. "Everyone except Miss Trask, Mart, Bob, Ned, and Brian."

"That's not fair!" Dan protested.

"It is, because they're going to get ready for the magic show," Trixie pointed out.

"Bob and Barbara have promised to sing. Barbara shouldn't have to help, either," Honey said.

"I don't mind. I always help with the dishes at home," Barbara insisted.

After the work was done, Miss Trask drew back the long curtains from the great view window that looked down over Central Park to the lighted buildings on the city's skyline. Gradually, one by one, the young people joined her and stood, fascinated. Ribbons of automobile lights wound in and out along the streets. Against the sky, the misted outlines of tall buildings glowed, alive with twinkling windows.

"If we'd just turn our backs," Ned said as Miss Trask snapped on half a dozen lamps and lit the electric fireplace, "we might almost be in the big kitchen of our home or at Happy Valley Farm."

"Or in Uncle Andrew's lodge in the Ozarks," Trixie added. "It's cozy. Imagine, in August, having the fireplace lighted!"

"It's an illusion," Miss Trask said. "It's just light. I didn't turn on the heat. The logs are imitations."

"It's just as cozy as if they were real!" Jim said and settled down on the big sofa. "I'm ready to be entertained. Here's a front row seat, Trixie!" He patted the seat beside him.

Ned brought in a small table, covered it with a black cloth, then set a bowl, a black box, and some other strange props on it.

Bob and Barbara took up their guitars and ran some eerie chords up and down the strings for a fanfare. Bowing, smiling, Mart stepped out on the stage and tapped with his stick for attention.

"Ladies and gentlemen, you are about to be entertained by the world's most famous magician. But if this trick works, I'll be more surprised than you are. Watch carefully. You may be able to find out how to do it. If you do, let *me* know."

Mart took out a Coke bottle and put it in a paper bag. "This is the favorite beverage of a lot of kids, but some may prefer another kind. Anyone for root beer?"

"I'd like one," Bob said, going to Mart's side.

Mart snapped his fingers, mumbled some magic words, reached into the paper bag, and drew out the same Coke bottle!

"Something must have gone wrong," he said, an

exaggeratedly worried look on his face. "I must have said the wrong word. Who wants lemon soda?"

"I do," Brian said and appeared at Mart's other side.

"You'll have it, sir," Mart said. "Abracadabra!" He snapped his fingers, reached into the bag, and brought out the very same bottle of Coke.

"Well, so much for that trick," he said and put the bottle of Coca-Cola back in the bag, slapped the paper flat, rolled it up, and threw it over his shoulder.

"Heavens, Mart, where did the bottle go?" Barbara called in amazement.

"That's the trick!" Mart said gleefully. "I made it disappear!"

"Now, friends," he went on, "whenever I do this trick—and I learned it from a famous Oriental magician—bands play, people shout, and ushers walk up the aisle with bouquets of flowers for me. Watch carefully. It puzzles me more than it will puzzle you. I have here a five-dollar bill. I borrowed it from Miss Trask. I'll tear a corner from it, see? I'll give the corner to Honey. Anyone knows that a torn corner can only be matched to a bill from which it has been torn. Do you see that envelope Bob is holding way across the room? You will agree that I haven't touched it?"

The members of the audience nodded.

"Well, then, if Miss Trask will please take the envelope from Bob's hand and open it, she will find a five-dollar bill with the corner torn. Right, Miss Trask?"

"Yes, I have it here." Miss Trask held up the bill.

"Now, if Honey will hand the corner I tore to Miss

93

Trask, she will see if it fits. Does it, Miss Trask?"

"Perfectly! How *did* you do it? I was watching you all the time!"

"I held that corner all the time, too," Honey said.

"It's nothing. I even amaze myself." Mart swelled out his chest.

The show went on. Mart made a bowl of water disappear, but not till he'd tried twice and spilled some. He knotted silks, shook the knots out of them, struck metal hoops together into a chain, and shook them apart. As his show went on, he told funny stories and kept up a continuous patter that left all his watchers baffled.

After he bowed to great applause and left the stage with his faithful helpers, Ned, Bob, and Brian, Miss Trask slipped away to the kitchen and returned with a tray of soft drinks and a huge bowl of cheese popcorn. "We couldn't pop it in an artificial fireplace, but it *is* good. Try it!"

"Now, Mart Belden," she said, after she had passed around the popcorn, "I want to know how you did those tricks. I could see what you were doing, but I don't know how."

"Sorcery, occultism, necromancy, wizardry, black magic . . . you couldn't possibly understand or perform the feats I have performed," Mart said airily. "You just aren't one of the gifted ones. Say, Trixie, that reminds me. What about that prophecy that woman gave you at Kennedy? Weren't you supposed to come up with some kind of good fortune? You

94

couldn't call those two who have been following us good fortune, could you?"

"No, but lots of other things come before the fortune in the prophecy," Trixie reminded him.

"There's so much junk in it I can't remember a tenth of it. There wasn't anything about that thief today."

"There *is*, Mart," insisted Trixie. "I know the prophecy by heart. 'Watch out for thieves; they're everywhere,' it said."

"Heavens, I'm shivering," Barbara said. "All this magic, thieves following, and prophecies! It's wonderful! It's fabulous the way it's turning out! Say, Mart, why don't you answer Miss Trask's question? How *did* you do those tricks? I'm baffled!"

"It was simple; I might just as well tell you. Here's the Coke bottle, for instance." He produced the paper bag, opened it, and took out a flattened imitation Coke bottle. "I bought it at the magic store."

"I could tell it was some kind of a fake bottle," Trixie said, "but that trick with the five-dollar bill really threw me."

"That was easier than the other," Ned said. "You see, before we came here, Mart took a five-dollar bill and tore off the corner. Then he palmed it—vanished it."

"Palmed? Vanished?" Diana asked.

"Yeah. He rolled up the corner he had torn from the five-dollar bill he put in the envelope. Then, when he tore off the corner of *another* bill on the stage, he palmed that corner and gave to Honey the one he had previously torn from the bill in the envelope. See?"

"Oh, that was sneaky!" Trixie said admiringly.

"Of course. All magic is sneaky," Ned agreed. "But it's mystifying. I bought some of the same junk Mart did, and I'm going to be 'Neddo the Necromancer' when I get back to Rivervale."

"Isn't that about enough magic?" Mart said and dropped into an easy chair. "Entertain me, slaves!" he commanded Bob and Barbara. "Guitar music! Song!"

Bob and Barbara jumped to their feet, salaamed in front of Mart, then sat side by side on chairs in the middle of the room. They strummed their guitars to see if they were in tune, then sang sweetly:

> "Out on the prairie, stars in the sky,
> Soft wind a-cryin', askin' me why,
> Why I'm so lonely, why, oh, my, why?
> Why, said the wind to me, why do you sigh?
> Far from my sweetheart, lone, all alone,
> Wind asked me why,
>   and the wind should have known."

Bob and Barbara increased the tempo of their accompaniment.

> "A man's only half a man
> Without his love,
> Without his love, without his love
> Held close to his heart.
> A man's only half a man,
> And the littlest part."

"It's lovely!" Miss Trask said when the twins had finished. She clapped louder than any of the others.

"I never heard that melody before, or the words."

"We made it up," Barbara said shyly. "Bob did most of it."

"Sing another!" they all shouted. "Please!"

Bob and Barbara changed places. She pulled her chair a little back of Bob's. Then they sang a song that jingled:

> "Andy went to town to buy a gift to send his lady.
>   Couldn't find a thing to please, no matter what he paid.
>   He walked up one street, down another,
>   Looked in windows, said he druther
>   Go back home and make a present for his sweet.
>
> "Oh, Andy took the sunshine, mixed it with the blue
>   Sky that spread above him, added white clouds, too.
>   Andy took the perfume from sage and mountain pine,
>   From alkali tossed into dust his pony's feet sent flyin'.
>   He boxed it and addressed it—Back Bay, Boston, Mass.
>
> "Then waited, sure for certain
>   his gift would bring his lass.
>   Sure enough!
>   The day that she received it,
>   Andy's lady fair
>   Took a plane to Phoenix,
>   Wired him to meet her there.
>   So . . .
>   It isn't the cost of a present, you see,
>   That matters to ladies; it's just the idee."

Before the Bob-Whites had a chance to applaud the song, they realized that someone had been knocking hard at the door.

Miss Trask went to open it.

A man stood there. "I'd like to speak to the Westons," he said. "My name is Meredith. I live just down the hall."

"There are no Westons here," Miss Trask said. "I'm afraid you must have gotten the wrong apartment number."

Mr. Meredith looked puzzled. "The Westons aren't here? I was sure I heard them playing. I'm with Celebrity Broadcasting, and the Westons, brother and sister, sing on one of my evening shows."

Miss Trask smiled. "Bob and Barbara Hubbell have been playing and singing. They're visiting here from Iowa." She gestured toward the twins seated in the living room.

Mr. Meredith looked embarrassed. "Oh, I *have* made a mistake. I could have sworn— Well, those two sound enough like the Westons to *be* the Westons. Have you ever been on television?" he asked the Hubbell twins.

"Only locally—in Des Moines," Bob answered.

"Are you going to live in New York now?"

"No, sir, we're just visiting for a few days."

"Too bad. I could use you." He turned to Miss Trask. "Are you their mother?"

Miss Trask smiled. "No, but I surely wish I were. Why?"

"I'd like to have them appear on our amateur program the day after tomorrow," Mr. Meredith said. "It might turn out to be well worth your while, Barbara and Bob. Do you want to try?"

The Bob-Whites stared at him in astonishment and delight.

"We'd love it; wouldn't we, Bob?" Barbara answered finally. "If you think we're good enough."

"I do think so," Mr. Meredith answered. "See you at the studio?"

The twins nodded vigorously.

Mr. Meredith wrote something on a card and stepped inside the room to hand it to Bob. "This is your card of introduction. I'll run along now. I'm sorry I barged in. Forgive me. I really could have sworn. . . ." He backed out of the door.

"Jeepers!" Mart said. "A national hookup! You'll knock 'em dead!"

"Thanks for thinking so," Barbara said. "Heavens, Bob, just imagine!"

A Queer Coincidence • 9

NEXT MORNING the telephone jangled as Miss Trask was getting breakfast.

"I'll get it!" Trixie called and took up the receiver. "Hello?" She rattled the button and answered again, puzzled: "Hello?"

"That's funny!" Trixie said, puzzled. "I was sure there was someone on the line, but nobody said a thing."

"Wrong number!" Honey said. "It happens all the time. People have a hard time remembering seven or eight digits when they look them up in the directory."

"I'm not so sure it was a wrong number," Trixie said thoughtfully. "My dad said once that thieves sometimes telephone to learn if anyone is at home.

We didn't hear one word from the police about the robber who was here."

"I told you before that as long as that thief didn't steal anything, you probably won't hear a word," Dan said. "I don't think that call was anything but a wrong number. Let's all wade into the waffles Miss Trask is making. Boy, look at the real maple syrup, too!"

"You eat this waffle you just baked, Miss Trask. I'll bake the rest of them. I know you're in a hurry to get to the hospital, since you didn't go last evening." Trixie poured batter into the waffle iron, then waited for it to brown.

"Where are you going today?" Miss Trask asked as Jim pulled out her chair and pushed the syrup jug where she could reach it.

"Bedloe's Island. Statue of Liberty!" Barbara and Bob chorused. "I've wanted to see it all my life!" Barbara added breathlessly.

"Not *quite* that many years!" Mart grinned. "It's not 'Bedloe's Island' now, either, Barbara. It's 'Liberty Island,' but nobody calls it that."

"Whatever you call it, that's where we're going," Trixie answered gaily. "If we get back from there in time, we may go tea dancing, then have a light dinner. We want to go to the Empire State Building for a view of the city at night."

The Bob-Whites and their friends had to scramble for the subway to get to Battery Park in time for the nine o'clock boat. It ran only on the hour, and Jim thought they would need to spend at least two hours on the island to see everything that they wanted to see.

They boarded the small ferry just as it tooted its last call. Soon they were bobbing in the bay. From the rail they looked back on the shoreline and the sparkling towers of mid-Manhattan. The bright sun of midday tinted the roofs with gold until they blended in one shining blur.

In the bay, husky little tugs steamed and snorted as they nudged huge barges on their way or pulled freighters into place. The water was alive with craft of every kind, from small powerboats to huge liners heading for the open sea.

"I wish I had as many eyes as a fly or a spider," Barbara said as she ran from one side of the ferry to the other, excitedly calling out to Bob the new things she saw.

"I'll settle for the sight of the Statue herself, over there ahead of us," Ned said.

"Isn't she huge?" Barbara sighed. "Isn't she perfectly beautiful?"

"I've seen it many times, but every time is a new thrill," Honey agreed. "Look, the ferry's stopping."

"I'm going way up to the very top," Bob said, "to that little balcony right under the torch. See it up there?"

Dan shook his head. "Nope, you're not. Nobody can go up there anymore. I don't know why. But don't worry, Bob, because you can see just as much from that balcony that runs around her head."

As they drew near the great base of Liberty, Jim said, "Bartholdi, the man who designed the statue, had a genius for symbolism. Look at her bare feet. They show her humility. The broken chains of slavery lie next to her feet. In her left hand she holds a tablet symbolizing our Declaration of Independence."

"I don't see how you can tell all those things from here," Barbara said. "Her feet are so huge they're all I can see."

"I can't see anything but her feet right now, myself," Jim said, smiling. "I know the other things are there, though."

They went inside the base of the statue and looked around eagerly.

"Let's climb up to the first balcony," Mart suggested, "or maybe you girls can take the elevator and we'll meet you there."

"No, you don't," Jim said. "We'll all climb, or we'll all take the elevator. We can't lose sight of the girls for a minute, after the queer things that have been happening."

"I guess you're right," Brian agreed. Trixie heard him say under his breath to Jim, "I didn't like that odd telephone call this morning . . . no one on the line."

Trixie couldn't hear what Jim answered. She had no time to ask, however, because the others were on their way up the stairs. At different levels there were pictures of the sculptor Bartholdi and the different stages in the development of the statue and its site.

"Boy, is that a view!" Bob said as they went out to the first balcony. "See the midget tugs and—gosh —look at the country all around here!"

"Yes. You can see Manhattan, of course, and Jersey City, over there." Brian pointed them out. "Brooklyn, Hoboken—what are you laughing at, Ned?"

"Some of the names. Hoboken is funny-sounding. So is Weehawken. And Tonawanda. Spuyten Duyvil . . . there's a doozer for you!"

"I suppose you think some of the Iowa names didn't sound funny to us—Pottawattamie, Maquoketa, Winneshiek. . . ." Jim smiled.

"Maybe they do sound odd if you aren't used to them," Ned agreed. "They're all Indian names."

"So are the New York State names . . . all except Spuyten Duyvil. It's Dutch. It means just what it sounds like—'spite the devil.'"

"Are you two going to sit down and discuss semantics, or are we going to have fun?" Mart asked.

"If that's what we're discussing, we'll stop it right now," Ned said. "I'll have to ask Bob the meaning of that word."

"Never mind. He tripped me up once, and that's enough," Mart said. "It's one hundred and sixty-eight steps up to the next balcony. Who wants to go?"

"I do," Trixie said quickly.

"So do we!" the rest of the group called. But when Diana saw the narrow spiral stairway, she hung back from the others.

"Oh, come on, Di!" Trixie begged. "If you don't go, we'll have to stay down here. Jim will go ahead of you and one of the other boys right back of you. It's not so bad."

It wasn't too bad, but Diana was shaking when she reached the top. She clung to Mart's arm as they walked around the small balcony.

"I'll bet we can see as far as Des Moines!" Barbara exclaimed breathlessly. "Which direction is Westchester County?"

"You can't really see it now," Brian explained. "It's way over there past the tip of Manhattan. You'd better tie your scarf, Barbara. There's really a wind up here."

"Everything's so gorgeous, I don't mind the wind," Barbara cried, standing on tiptoe. "See all those people streaming from the ferry. There must be thousands of visitors on this island now . . . and thousands of boats and barges and steamships and everything out there in the bay. They all look like beetles—even the big steamships!"

"Manhattan looks like something I used to build with blocks," Bob said. "Gosh, it's really neat!"

"I doubt if people in Manhattan would use that adjective to describe it," Trixie said. "It shines like a diamond necklace, seen from here, though. That's Ellis Island over north of us."

For a long time the Iowans, engrossed, watched the movement in the water far below. Finally, reluctantly, they were aware that it was time to leave.

"The ferry is just backing away from Battery Park on its way over here. If we want to get it going back, we'd better scram down these stairs," Mart said.

"And knock over a hundred people coming up?" Jim asked. "Watch your step, everybody!"

The Bob-Whites and their visitors crowded as far over to one side of the steps as they could. When they reached the lower balcony, they had to wait nearly ten minutes before they had a chance to go on down the stairs. Then they raced to the ferry, which puffed importantly while it waited.

As they lined up along the rail on the return trip, four sturdy tugs escorted a huge Cunard liner across the bay. Streamers of curled paper still trailed from its promenade deck, tributes from friends who had seen passengers off on a cruise. The band on deck played lustily, and, as the big ship slowly passed the small ferry, the passengers shouted and waved.

It was after one o'clock when the ferry stopped.

"I'm starving," Honey announced. "Shall we have our lunch at a restaurant in Battery Park?"

"You mean not go to that place where we can dance?" Barbara's voice sounded disappointed.

"Of course we'll dance!" Jim assured her. "Here's a candy bar to keep you from starving, Honey. It's my last one, so you may have to divide it."

Honey took the candy bar eagerly, stripped off its wrapper, broke it, and offered it to the others.

"Shove it in your mouth in a hurry, if we're going to make the train!" Mart suggested. "Look at that gang making for the subway station. Watch out there, sir. Watch where you're going!"

A shabbily dressed man had shoved Trixie rudely against the stone wall of the subway entrance, then pushed ahead of her to block her way on the stairs.

"Hey there, you!" Jim called. He and Brian and Ned closed in on the man just as he made a quick grab for Trixie's purse. The man missed it, cursed, turned, and ran down the steps two at a time. Jim and Brian took off after him, shouting back to the other boys to stay close to the girls.

"It was no use!" they reported, panting, when they rejoined their friends at the foot of the stairs after a few moments.

"He just disappeared," Jim said, frustrated. "Trixie, I believe it was your friend with the scar."

"It *couldn't* be," Trixie moaned, her voice trembling. "How could he possibly know we were going to be here?"

"Keep on walking, kids," a man back of them said impatiently. "Forget that guy! He didn't get your purse, miss, did he? Call yourself lucky. Thieves hang out at these entrances. They're after tourists like you. If you dangle your purse at the end of your arm, don't blame anyone but yourself if a thief gets it. If you lived in New York, then you'd know what to expect."

"We *do* live in New York," Jim said crisply. Then he ignored the man and urged the others to hurry.

"See, now?" Trixie exclaimed as they huddled close

107

together in subway seats. "That's more of the prophecy coming true!"

Mart was unconvinced. "I sure don't recall anything as sensible as 'Statue of Liberty' or 'Bedloe's Island' in that stuff the Mexican woman wrote."

"You don't?" Honey quoted softly, "'Watch out for thieves; they're everywhere.'"

"Gosh, Honey, Trixie already quoted that about the thief who broke into the apartment." Mart smiled.

"*If* you weren't so impatient, *if* you didn't interrupt, *if* you'd listen for a minute, Honey would tell you the rest. Go on, Honey," Trixie urged.

"Watch out for thieves; they're everywhere,
At home, on island, dead beasts' lair."

"Now, what do you say to that, Mart Belden? 'On island,' the prophecy said. We just left an island, didn't we?"

"You win, Trix. But I still say it's just a queer coincidence."

"Didn't he call our stop?" Jim asked. The group jumped to their feet, hurried through the door onto the platform, and filed up the stairs.

Trapped! • 10

IT WAS AFTER TWO o'clock when Trixie and her friends arrived at the tearoom in the hotel east of Central Park.

Ned held the door open as they went into the lobby.

"Oh, boy, listen to that music!" Mart exclaimed.

"It's Freddy Fedder's piano. Gosh, I've got one of his records back home!" Ned exclaimed. "Man! And that's Max Meader on the trumpet!"

Barbara stood listening breathlessly. "Max Meader!" she sighed. "Isn't this wonderfully wonderful? That crowd! The music! And something smells wonderful, too."

"It's food, at last," Honey sighed.

The huge room was almost filled with young people

—some dancing, some sitting at tables eating or sipping soft drinks.

"They have a buffet here where we help ourselves," Trixie explained. She led the way toward a long table. "Don't hold back. Take all you want, because one price includes everything."

Part of a huge ham stood ready to slice. Many kinds of cheese, jars of peanut butter, and jelly were available for sandwiches. There were hot hamburgers, crispy French fried potatoes, catsup, mayonnaise, plenty of lettuce, pickles, cookies, cakes, milk, Cokes. It was an array of food that stretched the length of the long buffet.

A man on drums beat out a staccato background for trumpet and piano. The twins' feet shuffled to the rhythm as they moved along the line, filling their plates.

"You were the one who said he didn't want to waste time dancing," Barbara told Ned, right behind her, as his feet, too, caught the tempo.

"Put dancing and food together and watch me work!" Ned chuckled. "Cake, Barbara?" He put a huge piece of chocolate cake on Barbara's plate.

Luckily they found a table big enough that they could all sit together. Laughing, humming the music, they crowded around it. When they had finished eating, they danced.

The girls went breathlessly from one partner to another, excited, laughing. "Isn't it wonderful?" Barbara's eyes danced as Brian took her from Mart and whirled her around. "New York's the most wonderful place in the whole world!"

"I guess New York does seem wonderful," Jim admitted later as Barbara, exhausted, dropped into her chair beside him and sat dreamily sipping a Coke. "I imagine, though, if you lived near the city all the time, as we do, you'd be just like Trixie. She can take fun for a while; then she has to get to work on something serious."

Mart snorted. "Boy, does she have you dazzled, Jim! You should hear her when Moms wants her to dust the house or help with the cooking."

"Gosh, why should she have to do that, when she can catch a gang of thieves like those you told us were after the antiques in your show?" Bob asked admiringly.

"And show up Di's phony uncle the way she did," Ned added. "Here, just let me touch you, won't you, please, Miss Sherlock?"

"Stop it!" Trixie insisted, embarrassed. "The Bob-Whites all helped on those projects. It just seems that I get the credit, and I don't deserve it. Save all the applause till I find out who those men are who are after my Incan idol—and why. That's a puzzler. Come on, Dan; you haven't danced at all, and this time you're dancing with me!"

Dan protested. "I haven't danced because I don't know how. You know I can't, Trixie."

"I know you can't if you don't try. Come on!" Trixie waited until he got to his feet and took her hand.

"It's your funeral . . . your feet's funeral, anyway," Dan said.

While they were dancing, the boys carried the plates and other things to the back of the room and piled them on trays to be washed.

"I sure wish we had a hangout like this in Rivervale or even in Des Moines," Ned said. "They don't charge very much for all this, either."

"That's because all the kids pitch in and help," Jim explained. "They don't have to have any waiters. They put their money in good food and good music. The guy who started this place has about a dozen of them around the city now. They're catching on all over the country . . . nightclubs just for teen-agers."

"Don't you think we'd better be shoving off?" Dan asked as he and Trixie came back to the table after the dance. "We said we'd be back for an early dinner. Miss Trask may be expecting us."

"She won't expect us till she sees us," Honey said knowingly.

"We're going to stop at the Museum of Natural History, though, on our way home, aren't we?" Bob asked. "It may be our only chance, with all the other things you've planned for us to do."

"Sure thing, we'll stop," Jim assured him. "We wouldn't pass up a chance to show you a ghostfish like the ones we found in that Ozark cave this summer. This one will be in a jar, though, and pickled. Let's get going!"

A little tired from all the dancing, the group walked

slowly across the park to the big red brick museum building.

"We'll go right up to the fourth floor, because we don't have much time before closing," Brian said and led the way to the elevator.

"Gosh, is it a giant fish you're going to show us?" Bob asked as they went through the dinosaur room and began to walk toward the alcove where the fish were exhibited.

"Hardly. The fish we want to show you is about three inches long." Mart measured the distance with his two hands. "Look at that boy, though! He's more than three inches long! I'd hate to meet him wandering around in the woods!"

The skeleton of a huge *Gorgosaurus* faced them, its short front feet upraised, a giant lizardlike tail trailing. Its huge head was set on a long neck, and a light exposed the bones and great eye sockets.

"That baby roamed all over North America several million years ago. There's a *Tyrannosaurus rex* over there." Mart pointed to another exhibit. "He was a meat-eater. Right beyond him are a duck-billed dinosaur and a horned one. Over in the corner is a skeleton of a *Pterosaur*."

"Not really!" Dan pretended amazement. "You left me behind a long time ago, Mart. What is the what-do-you-call-it you just said?"

"A flying reptile."

Ned was fascinated. "I know where I want to spend some time when I come back to New York, if we get

113

to come back. Right here. I want to explore all four floors."

"While you're doing that, Barbara and I will go to the Metropolitan Museum of Art," Diana told him. "Right now, though, we'd better take a quick look at that ghostfish, then go back to the apartment."

"It's right here." Brian stopped in front of a series of shelves. There were dozens of jars containing rare fish suspended in alcohol. "There's one that looks just like our little contribution to science—the one we found in the Ozark cave."

A jar stood on a small square pedestal. Inside, in alcohol, there was a fish so white it seemed transparent. The legend under it read:

> BLIND CAVE FISH. In the process of evolution, because its life-span is spent in complete darkness underground, the cave fish loses its sight. Then, through generations of lack of use, its eyes disappear.

A printed card stood against the jar. It related the recent discovery of a similar fish in "Bob-White Cave" in the Ozarks and listed the names of the club members underneath.

"How come my name is there?" Dan asked.

"You're a Bob-White, aren't you, Dan?" Trixie reminded him.

"One for all," Mart chanted. "All for one."

"Well, that's just too wonderfully wonderful!" Barbara exclaimed. "To think you knew how important that little fish was!"

"We didn't know exactly," Jim said. "Trixie read about it in a magazine when we were at her Uncle Andrew's lodge in the Ozark Mountains, and she led us on the hunt for it."

"We all worked together on that project," Trixie said modestly. "I never do anything by myself. Honey and I both know that our detective agency just could not exist without help from all the Bob-Whites. It's a long story about the fish. We'll tell you all about it later."

"Seems to me it'd be a lot easier to discover something the size of that *Gorgosaurus*," Bob remarked.

"Except that he was found all in pieces," Mart told Bob, "some of them not even as big as our little fish."

"I'd like to take another look at those 'sauruses.' Does anyone mind?" Bob asked.

"Me, too," Barbara echoed. "Remember that movie, Bob, where all those big prehistoric animals were moving around on earth? Do we have time, Jim, to take another look at the skeletons?"

"You'll have to make it snappy. Come on, gang, let's start toward the exit. Bob and Barbara can look at the prehistoric exhibit again on our way out."

Trixie and Honey were on the other side of the big room, completely absorbed in a great glass case filled with skeletons of deep-sea fish. They didn't hear what Jim said or see the rest of the crowd leaving.

"How would you like to encounter something like that in the dead of night?" Honey asked, pointing through the glass to a skeleton fish, almost all mouth.

115

Its great jaws were open to display two long rows of sharp, ugly teeth.

"Right next to the skeleton, too, see, Trixie—a picture of the way that fish looks in real life. Heavens! It has luminous eyes and a real cavern for a mouth!"

Trixie crouched down to peer through the glass. She shuddered as she saw the pictured monster's eyes gleaming. Then she realized she was gazing right into the eyes of a man looking into the case from the other side.

The face was that of the sleek-haired man they had seen at the United Nations!

Honey saw him at the same moment. She seized Trixie's hand tightly, and they both looked around for the rest of their crowd.

"They're gone!" Trixie gasped. "Honey, some of the lights have been turned off! It must be closing time! Where did Jim go?" Her voice fell to a whisper. "Did you see that awful man?"

Honey squeezed Trixie's hand tightly in answer. "Let's get out of here fast!"

They looked around frantically. Far down the corridors more lights went off. The girls, desperate, plunged madly around the great glass case, practically into the arms of the stranger!

"It's my little friends from the Peruvian exhibit, isn't it? How lucky for you you found me here!" He chuckled softly.

Trixie, almost taken off her feet with the impact, recovered herself, her eyes seeking escape.

"It's lucky, young ladies, because if you will only follow me, you will discover you are not to be locked in. I know a quick way out of the building. Just follow me!" He grasped Trixie's arm with one hand and Honey's arm with the other and tried to pull them along with him.

Angrily they struggled to free themselves, almost speechless with fright. "Jim!" Trixie called in a shrill voice. "Jim! Where are you? Where is *everybody?* Mart! Brian! Dan! Jim! Jim! Help!"

The man held tight to their arms. "Young ladies! Young ladies! I'm trying to help you!"

Honey's voice rose pleadingly. "Somebody help us! Anybody! Don't lock the doors!"

Fighting fiercely, Trixie echoed, "Help! Help! Jim —Brian—help!"

There was a sound of hurrying feet. Lights flashed. The man quickly released the girls, smoothed his tie, and set his hat at a jaunty angle as Jim rushed down the corridor shouting, "We're coming, Trix—Honey— hold on!"

The other Bob-Whites followed closely after him. A worried-looking attendant hurried in, protesting, apologizing.

Before Trixie could speak, the dark-haired man said in an oily voice, "The little girls were worried. They thought they were being locked in. I wanted to show them another exit. They became excited. I only wanted to help!"

Jim, evidently puzzled when he found someone with

the girls, said brusquely, "Thanks! We'll take care of things here now. Thank you very much."

The man bowed with exaggerated politeness, backed off, turned, and hurried down the hall. Honey and Trixie, so relieved to see their friends, didn't even see him leave.

"Didn't you hear the warning bell sound?" the attendant demanded sharply. "The museum closes promptly at five o'clock. It's fifteen minutes *after* now."

"Of course they didn't hear the bell, or they'd have left when they should," Jim said. "I'd suggest you calm down a little. Can't you see that the girls have been frightened?"

"I raised my voice without thinking," the attendant said in apology. "I guess it was because it scared me, too, to think someone might have been locked in. Now, if you'll all leave, I'll go ahead and close up."

Out on the street, Trixie found her voice again. "We should have followed that man, Jim. He was the same one we saw at the gift shop in the United Nations. He tried to *hold* us—tried to drag us along with him!"

"He said he was trying to help us," Honey added. "Said he wanted to show us another exit."

"Why on earth didn't you speak up before he left?" Jim asked, his face burning red. "We thought you were crying out because you were afraid of being locked in. I did think something sounded phony. . . ."

"So did I. Boy, are we a bunch of dumbbells!" Dan

looked right and left, up and down the street. "It's too late now, that's for sure!"

"The most awful things happen to you, Trixie." Diana shivered. "I don't ever want to be a detective."

"Well, I do." Trixie was very firm. "Anyway, maybe that man was trying to help. Mart says I'm always imagining things. Maybe the man thought he had two hysterical girls on his hands—"

"I doubt that very much," Jim said grimly. "Watch out for that bird if you ever see him again, Trixie. It looks to me as though we have *three* characters to beware of now: the pair who followed us home from Central Park, and the man you saw at the gift shop and here again today."

"I don't think so. I think the man we saw just now is the short one of the pair who followed us home."

Honey shook her head. "How could he have been at Bedloe's Island looking so dirty and shabby, then just now at the museum all dressed up, looking so sleek?"

"Maybe it was the *tall* man of the pair, then, who tried to take my purse over at the Island. . . . Oh, I'm so muddled and mixed-up right now I'm not sure about anything." Trixie threw up her hands. "What a day! I'll be glad to get back to our apartment."

Showstoppers · 11

WHEN THE DOORMAN opened the apartment door for them he said to Trixie, "Did your uncle find you?"

"My uncle?" Trixie asked, puzzled.

"Yes, miss. After you left this morning your uncle was here. When nobody was home, he asked if I knew where you were. I did, because you asked me about the nearest subway to the Liberty Island ferry, and then you asked me the hours of the Museum of Natural History. I told him I thought you might be intending to go both places. So he missed you, eh?"

"Yes . . . we didn't see my uncle." Trixie's face was very serious. Her companions suddenly sobered.

"What do you think now, Trix?" Mart asked as the group got into the elevator.

"I give up. Wait till Miss Trask hears what has happened."

"It's that Incan idol," Miss Trask said grimly when they told her about the man who pretended to be Trixie's uncle and about their encounter at the museum. The Bob-Whites and their guests were seated around the dining room table, finishing a delicious dinner prepared by Miss Trask.

"I'm sure of that, but why?" Trixie stood the little carved statue on the table in front of them. She shrugged her shoulders, perplexed.

"Not one of us can find anything concealed around his nibs," Brian explained to Miss Trask. "The woman at the gift shop in the United Nations Building told Trix it isn't a rare antique. Pass it over to Miss Trask. See if she can find anything different about it."

Miss Trask put on her glasses, ran her slender fingers carefully over the statue, then shook her head. "I can't find a thing. It's all solid wood."

"Not much chance for gold or jewels to be concealed in it that I can see," Jim said. "Some strange religious cults, though, get quite attached to their idols. Maybe this little chap guards their crops in their homeland, and the guys who want him back are afraid of a famine if he doesn't come back home."

"I'd give him back in a minute if I thought they were worried about that," Trixie said quickly. "We never have a chance to *ask* the men anything. If they'd come right out and say why they want the statue. . . . But instead they keep scaring the life out of us."

121

"Nix on giving it back," Dan said firmly. "I've seen a lot of crooks in this city, and I never yet saw one who wanted to steal for any reason except greed. That little idol means money in their pockets in some way."

"All of it's too much for me," Diana admitted.

"It's the most exciting thing in the world!" Barbara cried as Miss Trask refilled her glass with milk.

"Trixie will solve the mystery, sure as you're alive. Just give her time!" Ned said.

"Especially with that old Mexican woman's prophecy to guide her," Bob added.

"The less said about that, the better," Miss Trask suggested. "If that woman could see into the future, she'd be the wealthiest woman on earth."

"She hit everything right on the nose so far," Mart said. "Everything up till now, I mean. She missed on the man at the museum."

"How about 'Watch out for thieves; they're everywhere'?" Trixie quoted.

"You keep bringing that up all the time, as though it proved everything," Mart said impatiently. "It's worn out. Everybody watches out for thieves in New York."

"Just wait, Mart Belden. Wait one second. The next line goes on to say, 'At home, on island, *dead beasts' lair.*' Don't you see—all those dinosaurs and other skeletons at the museum?"

"Gosh!" Mart was stunned.

"After all that has happened today, don't you think you'd better not go to the Empire State Building tonight? Why don't you put it off till tomorrow night?" Miss Trask asked.

"Oh, no!" Trixie wailed. "Ned and the twins have counted on going tonight."

"It's okay. Barbara and Bob have the broadcast coming up tomorrow," Ned said.

"We really should practice a little tonight, Trixie," Bob told her. "It's pretty important to be on a national program. Barb and I sent our parents a telegram and told them to watch for it."

"All of the gang at Rivervale will be watching, you can be sure of that," Ned added. "Des Moines, too, I'll bet a cookie. And it'll be in the Des Moines *Register*, for sure."

"I didn't think about the practicing," Trixie said. "I suppose you will have to do that. . . . I guess we should put off going to the Empire State Building till afterward. You'll enjoy it more when the broadcast is off your minds. You won't be so nervous."

Bob straightened in his chair. "We're not nervous at all!"

"We are too, Bob Hubbell . . . at least I am. Heavens!" Barbara pushed her chair back into place. "After we help with the dishes, we'll get our guitars out and run over the new song we want to sing tomorrow."

"No dishes!" Dan stacked the plates. "It's our contribution to genius. We'll get a bang out of listening to you practice while we wash. Trixie and Honey had better be excused, too. Even if they won't admit it, they've had a bad scare."

"Then suppose we all go to bed early and get a good night's rest," Miss Trask said.

"Jeepers, not that!" Trixie protested.

When nine o'clock came, though, they were all beginning to yawn.

"Isn't it a glorious day?" Trixie exclaimed as they went out of the apartment building the next day.

"Right off the top shelf!" Mart stretched his arms and pounded his chest. "If we walk through the park leisurely, we'll just about get to Celebrity Broadcasting on time."

"And let Barbara and Bob carry their guitars all that distance?" Brian asked.

"They don't weigh a thing. I'd rather walk, wouldn't you, Barb?"

Barbara nodded her head. "Dan's carrying my guitar, anyway. I'd a million times rather walk than ride. There are so many things to see. Everything's so—"

"There goes Barbara's one adjective, 'wonderful,' " Bob said. Then he added quickly, "It is, too."

"Let me carry your guitar for you, Maestro Robert," Mart offered.

Bob handed it over. "You thought I wouldn't, didn't you? It wouldn't bother a monkey to carry it."

"Is there a hidden meaning in that remark?" Mart grinned.

"I was kidding. Give it back. I just wanted you to see how light it is."

124

"I will not. Everyone I pass thinks *I'm* the musician. I'll masquerade till we get to the studio."

"You won't have long to pretend," Dan said. "We'd better hustle. It's late."

They dodged in and out among the many people hurrying along Fifth Avenue. Poodles yapped furiously at them. Slender wolfhounds, on leashes, lifted their heads disdainfully. People seemed amused and stood aside as Trixie and her crowd ran, weaving in and out, to arrive, breathless, at the entrance to the studio. Trixie glanced at her watch and realized they had misjudged the time it would take to get there.

"Sorry!" the man at the door said. "No more tickets. You're just too late, kids. Try another day."

"Oh, no!" Barbara said, tears springing to her eyes. "We can't come another day. We're on the program today. See, here are our guitars."

"Sorry, miss. That's what everyone tells me. The room holds just so many. When it's full, it's full."

Trixie quickly reached into her pocket and pulled out the card that Mr. Meredith, the man from Celebrity Broadcasting Company, had given them the evening he heard Barbara and Bob play and sing. "Will this make any difference?"

"Lady, I'll say it will." The man whistled softly to himself. "Why didn't you say you were invited by the big brass himself?"

"Is Mr. Meredith 'Mr. Big'?"

"*Is* he!" the man answered. "Just follow me."

He led them down a corridor, through several doors

125

marked PRIVATE, until they ended within a few feet of the stage where the show was just ready for the air. "Here you are," he whispered. "We keep these places for the V.I.P.'s."

"What did he mean by that?" Barbara whispered to Dan as they quietly settled into their seats.

" 'V.I.P.' means 'Very Important People,' " Dan whispered back. "How about that?"

"Heavens! Imagine! It's—"

"Wonderful!" Bob finished for her.

"Shhh!" Brian warned. "The show's on the air."

The bouncy master of ceremonies stepped onto the stage in front of the microphone just as the clock hand arrived at one o'clock. After he had delivered his usual welcome talk to the audience, he introduced the first act. The lights in the small auditorium dimmed. A pretty teen-age girl sat down at the piano.

Obviously nervous, she played Chopin's "Polonaise" with growing control of her fingers. When she had finished, everyone applauded vigorously. The girl smiled gratefully.

A band of neighbor women using instruments made of various pots and pans followed. It was obvious that they played together for fun instead of harmony, and everyone laughed with them.

A black man sang "The Impossible Dream." His voice filled the small studio and beyond. The men in the control room twisted knobs to hold down the volume. When the singer had finished, the entire audience stood to applaud him.

126

"He'll be an opera star someday; see if he won't," Honey whispered.

Now it was Barbara and Bob's turn. The master of ceremonies called them to the stage. "These are two young folk singers from Iowa, Bob and Barbara Hubbell. One of our board members, Mr. Meredith, heard them sing and invited them to come here today. They write their own words and music. I'm looking forward to hearing them, just as I am sure you are. Let's give them a warm welcome."

Bob and Barbara smiled their appreciation of the applause, then as quickly as possible tuned their guitars and sang:

"The silver moon shone through the crepe myrtle tree,
  And a nightingale sang to my Mary and me.
  'We'll marry in August, my wee lass,' said I,
  'On a day the sun shines, with no clouds in the sky.'
        Shy she was, Mary,
        My little white dove,
        Golden-haired Mary,
        My only true love.

"In the moonlight she put her dear head on my shoulder,
  To give her consent; then I happily told her
  I'd build a small home for her, claim my sweet wife,
  And work for her, serve her throughout all my life.
        Shy she was, Mary,
        My little white dove,
        Golden-haired Mary,
        My only true love."

The twins stopped singing and drew beautiful, dreamy chords from their guitars, running softly up and down the scale till the audience burst into spontaneous applause. Then they sang the last verse slowly, wistfully.

"Alas, oh, my pretty one, alas, oh, my love,
Alas, oh, my sweetheart, my shy little dove.
She sickened and died; now the winter winds blow
O'er her grave and her cottage all covered with snow.
        Shy she was, Mary,
        Love of my life,
        Golden-haired Mary,
        My true love, my wife."

When the twins finished singing, everyone was quiet for a few moments. Then they clapped and whistled until Bob and Barbara bowed happily and went back to their seats.

After the show had ended, the master of ceremonies invited Bob and Barbara and their friends to his office backstage.

"You surely stopped the show, kids," he told them enthusiastically. "The Westons couldn't have done better—maybe not even as well. Wait a second till I get the phone." He answered, then listened for a few moments. "It's for you." He smiled broadly and handed the receiver to Bob.

As Barbara, all ears, listened, the master of ceremonies said with a broad grin, "It was the Folk Song Publishing Company calling. They wanted to know who owns the copyright to the song you sang."

"We wrote it," Barbara said quickly. "It didn't have to be cleared for public use."

"I wasn't worrying about that one bit. I'll be surprised if they aren't asking your brother to sign a contract with them to publish it."

Bob replaced the receiver slowly. He turned around to the Bob-Whites and his sister and Ned, his face a picture of mixed emotions. "They want to *pay* us to publish the song!"

"Hallelujah!" Mart took Barbara's hands and danced around the room. "Boy, is your fortune made!"

The master of ceremonies laughed. "Not quite. It might just catch on, though, and if you've written other songs, they'll want to see them, too; you can be sure of that. They pay on a royalty basis. It could mean a few dollars, and it could mean a lot more than that. Congratulations! Say, there goes the phone again."

The conversation was short. "It was Mr. Meredith," the man said with a smile.

"I hope he thought we were all right," Barbara said quickly.

"You bet he did, Barbara," the master of ceremonies said. "He said to tell you you were great. He repeated it twice, and that's something from Mr. Meredith. He said, too, that he'd talk to you later at home. It's liable to mean a contract for you. That'll bring you to New York."

"I'm afraid not," Bob spoke for the twins. "We're only in high school. It was a lot of fun to be on a big program at Celebrity. I hope the kids at home won't think we have the bighead. . . ."

129

"Nobody who knows you would think that!" Trixie said fiercely.

"Oh, no," echoed Honey.

"It'll be swell to talk to Mr. Meredith," Barbara declared. "He probably doesn't want to talk to us about a contract at all, but I know he can give us some good advice about what to do. We could sure use some money from royalties to help with our college fund."

Back in the apartment the telephone was ringing as they opened the door. Trixie ran across the room and answered.

"It's Moms!" she said, turning around to face the others, her eyes shining. "She heard the program. She wants to talk to you, Barbara."

Barbara talked for a minute, then handed the receiver to Bob.

"Isn't it great?" he said happily when he turned away. "Bobby talked to me, too. When he likes something he sure says so, doesn't he?"

"He's just as voluble when he doesn't," Mart said, laughing. "Did he say he liked the program?"

"He said his dog Reddy did."

"Wasn't it just wonderful of them to listen?"

"Moms said it was a shame our dad had to miss it," Trixie said.

"Didn't you tell her they're going to show it again on video tape tomorrow night?" Honey asked.

"I forgot. I'll have to call back. Your father will want to see it, too."

The telephone rang again.

"That'll be Mother," Honey said. "I know she was listening. I'll tell her about the video tape and tell her to call your mother, Trixie. She's probably had everyone around our house and grounds listening. Hello . . . Mother?"

Honey was right. When Mrs. Wheeler finished talking, Dan's uncle talked to him. To put a finishing touch to the excitement, a telegram came from Rivervale, Iowa.

"Gosh! Mom and Dad liked it, too," Bob said and handed the wire to Barbara. "I never in the world thought a little thing like singing a song or two would stir up such a breeze. I feel chesty enough to push over the Empire State Building. We *are* going there tonight, aren't we?"

Close Call · 12

THIS IS ONE DAY where nothing happened to carry out that fortune-teller's prophecy that impresses you so much," Mart told Trixie that evening as they prepared to leave for the Empire State Building.

"The day isn't over yet," Honey reminded him. "Is it, Trixie?"

Trixie didn't answer right away. At Mart's mention of the prophecy she took it from her purse. "There *is* something here about the broadcast," she announced triumphantly after a moment. "Listen to this!

> "When guitars play, thieves linger 'round,
> But not till later are they found."

"It sounds mysterious," Mart admitted. "They didn't show up, though, did they?"

" 'Not till later are they found,' " Trixie repeated.

"Oh, rubbish, you pay so much attention to that paper, you'd think Nostradamus himself wrote the prophecy," Mart said scornfully.

"Whoever *he* is," Trixie answered.

"Mart can tell you. He knows practically everything," Diana said proudly. "Anyway, if I thought that Mexican woman was right all the time, I'd be scared to go outside the apartment."

"There's something in what Diana says," Miss Trask remarked, overhearing the conversation. "I don't believe in the prophecy for one minute, but I do know that those two men, or three men, or whoever they are, seem to want that statue of Trixie's. I don't think she should be carrying it around with her all the time."

"They'll break in here and steal it if I leave it in the apartment."

"Let me take it—tonight, at least." Miss Trask's voice was anxious.

"Miss Trask! We don't want anything to happen to you any more than we want it to happen to Trixie," said Honey.

"Wait just a minute, everyone. I never go anyplace alone except to the hospital and back, and always in a taxi. Let me take it for the present. Tomorrow, why don't you look around that antique store where you bought it, Trixie, and see if you can discover anything more."

Reluctantly, Trixie gave the little idol to Miss Trask,

who tucked it into her purse. "If you don't find out anything more about it at the antique store tomorrow, don't you think we'd better turn it over to the police?" Miss Trask was obviously worried.

"No . . . no, I don't think so." Trixie shook her head. "It would just gather dust in the police station. The police have so many important things to look after. I've grown quite attached to the ugly little thing, anyway."

"Trixie's right about the police," Dan said. "I keep telling you that the police haven't a thing to work on in this case. His nibs is getting under *my* skin now. I have to find out who and what he is. Tomorrow I'll go with you, Trix, and do some sleuthing."

It wasn't much of a drive from Central Park West to the Empire State Building. Bob and Barbara rode with Jim and Trixie.

As they rounded the corner of the huge New York City Library, Jim pointed out the crouching lions guarding the entrance. "They're about as ferocious-looking as the Cowardly Lion in *The Wizard of Oz!*"

"Our English teacher at home told us the main reading room in that library is two blocks long. That couldn't possibly be true, could it, Jim?" Barbara turned her head to look back at the building.

"It could be," Jim answered. "The building covers a huge area. It has over seven million books on its shelves. You should go inside, Barbara. The Jefferson draft of the Declaration of Independence is on permanent exhibit there. We're coming to the Empire

134

State now. Seems as though we could have walked here faster. It wasn't your fault," Jim quickly told the driver. "It was a miracle you ever got through that traffic at all."

"Anyone who wants my job can have it at this time of night," the driver answered. "One thing you can remember: If you ride with me, you won't get your pocket picked. It happens all the time out there in that mob."

"That's one of the reasons we ride," Jim told him. "And thank you very much."

Inside the magnificent lobby, the twins and Ned gazed wonderingly at the strange modernistic mural on the walls, then at the mass of elevator doors.

"There must be a hundred elevators!" Bob said, awed. "Gosh!"

Trixie took Barbara's hand in hers. "Very near a hundred. When we get on one, it will go faster than any elevator you've ever been in in your life, Bob. Stand right here beside me, Barbara."

Trixie needn't have bothered for fear Barbara would be afraid. As the elevator shot up the granite shaft, the girl from Iowa cried out exultantly.

Not so Diana. "My ears!" she wailed. "They're popping so. What did you say, Trixie? I can't hear you."

"I said, 'Click your back teeth together, and that will stop the popping.'"

"I did it!" Diana said after a moment. "It's heavenly! Oh, there they go again!"

"Click them again. Then don't swallow!"

"I'm glad you told Di that," Bob said. "I had the same trouble with my ears. We must have gone a thousand feet a minute."

The passengers were discharged at the eightieth floor. There they took another elevator to the eighty-sixth floor, where the first balcony was located.

Diana was still shaking, so Trixie went with her into the enclosed area to wait till she calmed down a little. The others hurried out to the promenade, where they stood leaning against the rails, watching the quick-changing panorama far below. Trixie and Diana soon joined the group again.

"Over there against the sky is the tip of the Chrysler Building," Brian explained. "Beyond it, below, is the East River. You can see the cars crossing the Queens-boro Bridge."

"It's like a blur of ribbons trailed by tiny ants," Barbara said, awed. "What is that big space on the ground filled with lights like stars?"

"Central Park," Trixie told her. "Can you find the theater district?"

"I can!" Bob cried. "It's right down there, isn't it? Gosh! No wonder they call it the 'Great White Way.' Say, I wouldn't have missed this for a million. I'll bet we're higher up in the sky right now than we were on the plane that brought us to New York."

"What if a guy were up here on this floor and the elevators stopped running?" Ned asked. "Would he have to walk?"

"I guess so," Brian replied. "Some Norwegian ski

jumpers climbed up here just for kicks one time. It took them only twenty-five minutes."

"Plus all their wind for a week, I'll bet," Bob said with a laugh. "Did you just make that up, Brian?"

"Nope. It's true."

"Remember what the White Queen in *Alice in Wonderland* said?" Trixie asked. " 'I've believed as many as six impossible things before breakfast.' "

"Yeah? You can be sure she lived in Manhattan and not in England as the book says." Dan smiled.

Bob and Barbara and Ned walked around the high parapet two or three times, all the while asking the Bob-Whites to point out on the ground below some of the places where they had visited.

"There's a blaze of light like the north star right over us," Ned said. "Where is it coming from?"

"It's the Beacon of the Four Freedoms," Trixie answered. "Isn't it magnificent? When the weather is just right, those beams can be seen eighty miles away. Helen Keller came up here one time—she was deaf and blind, you know—but after she'd stood here, she went home and wrote an article. In it she said, 'The sun and stars are suburbs of New York, and I never knew it.' "

"She saw more here than many people who have their sight," Honey said thoughtfully.

"It makes an ordinary guy ashamed. . . . Say, let's go on up to the tower," Mart said. "You're really swinging in space up there—a hundred and two floors up!"

"Not me!" Diana said quickly. "I have the strangest

feeling that something terrible may happen!"

"It's because you're afraid of high places," Mart said. "Come on, Di; try to get over it."

"No. You can all go without me. I've never been up there, and I'm never going." She shuddered.

"I'll stay here with you," Trixie told her. "I've seen it often. I wouldn't want Barbara and Bob to miss it, though, if they aren't afraid. Di and I will look around here a little while, everybody, then meet you downstairs later."

"Don't go far from the elevators when you get downstairs, Trixie," Jim warned. "Even if you have to wait a long time for us, please stay right there."

"I will," Trixie promised. She put her arm around Diana protectively as the rest of her crowd scrambled for the elevator to take them to the tower.

While they were in the enclosed area, Diana was quite brave. "I never had any idea it could be so beautiful," she said. "It almost seems as though we were looking down from heaven, doesn't it? Trixie, I'm sorry you didn't go with the rest of them. I'm sorry I'm such a fraidycat."

"Don't think a thing about it. Lots of people much older than you have a fear of going up in high places. It has some kind of name—that fear—but I can't think of it. I've been to the tower many times, as I told you, so forget it. I'm not disappointed."

The two girls were so absorbed in the view from inside the windows that they didn't realize that the crowd had become much smaller. Many had gone to the higher parapet. Others apparently had seen all they wanted to see and had gone down on the elevators.

Aware, finally, of the lack of chatter and bustle around them, Trixie turned away from the windows to look about.

"Jeepers, we're almost the last ones up here!" she gasped. "How long have we been here? Maybe the others are waiting for us downstairs. We've just been standing here gazing so much we've forgotten the time. Let's go, Di!"

Diana whirled around. Then she caught Trixie's arm. "Don't look!" she warned. "But those two men over there look awfully suspiciously like— They are! Trixie, run! There's nobody up here but us and those men. Run! Run for the elevator!"

Trixie caught Diana's hand, and they both sprinted down the corridor.

"Where's the guard who's supposed to be here?" Trixie gasped as she ran.

"Way up there at the other end of the platform, I suppose," Diana cried. "Trixie, they're right back of us. It's those thieves! I know it is! Oh, I told you I knew something awful was going to happen. Run! Run faster!"

"It *is* those men!" Trixie gasped. Running, she called back to them, "*I don't have the statue!* I don't have it! Stay away from us."

The men caught up and dodged around them.

"They're in front of the elevator!" Diana's voice was

frantic. "They're going to stop us! Trixie! Don't go that way!"

"You got our idol! You give it back!" the taller man called, guarding the bell so the girls couldn't reach it to signal the elevator.

"I *don't* have it, I tell you. I gave it to somebody else! Get away from that bell! Let us out of here! Guard! Guard!" Trixie screamed.

"I don't see a soul in sight to help us," Diana moaned. "They'll kill us, Trixie!"

"Keep quiet!" Trixie commanded, realizing that Diana was almost hysterical. "The stairway, Di! Pretend we're going back along the corridor—here! Duck down here! Be quick!"

The girls pushed through the door leading to the stairway and flew down the steps. As they turned at the bend, they heard the door above them swish. The sound of footsteps followed.

"We—can't—possibly—run—like—this—for eighty—six —floors," Diana gasped. "Help! Help! Help!"

As they passed lighted floors, not a soul was visible. Above them, hardly a floor away, the men's heavy footsteps followed.

"In here!" Trixie cried and pulled Diana through one of the stair doorways, then down a hall. "We're sure to find someone here!"

"There's no one! We're lost! That—awful—statue!"

"Hush! We'll be all right. I don't think they followed us through that door. Walk quietly now, Di—hush— don't make a sound—softly—there! Look down the hall!

There's an office door open. In there, quickly!"

Trixie shoved Diana ahead of her through the half-opened door, closed it after her, and turned around to face two very puzzled cleaning women.

"See here, girls, you just get out of here. You're not supposed—"

"Oh, please let us stay!" Trixie cried. "Please! Lock the door! Some terrible men are following us—they followed us from the promenade deck—please!"

The older woman looked at her companion. "Well, now, the two little girls seem to need help. Two little girls—and nice-lookin' little girls they are, too—can't do a body any harm now, can they?"

"What's up?" the younger woman asked. She opened the door and peered down the hall. "There's no one after you that I can see."

"There *will* be! There surely will be as soon as they know we've slipped away!" Diana trembled.

"Well, they're not goin' to harm you, whoever they are!" The older woman snapped the lock on the door. "Calm down, darlin's. There'll be no one harmin' you. I'll just call the maintenance department. Sit down there, the two of you. We'll get to the bottom of this in no time at all."

She telephoned to another floor, and in a few minutes a service elevator stopped far down the hall. A man from the maintenance department came to the door.

Trixie, unnerved now that help had come, told her story in a shaking voice.

The man and two women listened as she related everything that had happened since she bought the statue.

"I wasn't sure before that it *was* the idol they were after, but I am now," Trixie said positively.

"You're right. They'll stop at nothing now to get it," the maintenance man said. "How does it happen that two young girls like you are out by yourselves at this time of night?"

"We're not by ourselves," Trixie told him. "Six boys and two other girls went up to the tower. I thought I told you that. They're waiting downstairs for us right now. Where do you think those men went?"

"It's anyone's guess," the man said. "Come with me now, on the service elevator. If there *were* men following you, and if they're still going down the stairs, maybe we'll get to the first floor ahead of them."

Trixie and Diana thanked the cleaning women and went with the man. He operated the service elevator himself and slowed the pace so he could glance down each floor as he passed.

When the elevator stopped at the first floor, Jim and Brian were pacing up and down impatiently in front of the passenger elevators. When Trixie ran up to Jim, he threw his arm around her. "I thought you were lost! Oh, Trixie, I didn't know what had happened to you! Mart's up on the eighty-sixth floor now. We have the whole building staff looking for you!"

As quickly as she could, supplemented by the comments of Diana and the maintenance man, Trixie told

142

the waiting, worried group what had happened.

Before long Mart came back. Several men were with him. A crowd had gathered and even elevator men stopped to listen. A policeman dispersed the onlookers. "Now, let's hear what this is about," he said.

Wearily, Trixie and Diana told their story again. The policeman made notes. The maintenance man made notes. The elevators resumed their continuous up, down, up, down.

There was no sight of the two men. They were not seen again that night, either, though the maintenance staff searched each floor.

Finally, exasperated, the maintenance men turned the matter over to the policeman.

"There's only one thing to do, the way I see it," the officer announced. "It's this. The hands of the police are tied unless they have some real description of the men. All you seem to know now is that one is tall and one is short and has a scar."

"I know that," Trixie said unhappily. "No matter where *I* saw them, I'd know them, but I can't describe them any better than I have. What makes it even more puzzling is that we're so mixed up about the short man. He either looks different almost every time he shows up, or there is a third man. It's so confusing."

"Then do this. The minute you catch sight of them anyplace, call a policeman. We can hold anyone as a suspect for twenty-four hours if we have a shred of evidence. They've given us the slip tonight. It's not hard to figure out how this happened. There are

143

thousands of tourists in the building right now. You just happened, by some freak of chance, to be up there in a slack time. For a second you were the only ones on that observation deck, aside from those men. When you escaped, they could have gone back up there and lost themselves in the crowd coming down. Okay, sister, keep your eyes open, and remember what I said. In the meantime, you'd better stick close together, all of you in a group."

Dr. Joe · 13

OUTSIDE THE EMPIRE State Building the Bob-Whites, sobered, crowded into cabs. Even the badges the Iowa visitors wore so proudly, "I've been to the top!" didn't take the worried frown from Trixie's forehead.

"So many things have happened to spoil everything for you," she told them. "Now tonight was the worst of all."

"What do you mean? You've said that before. It's the thrill of a lifetime for Ned and Barbara and me!" Bob exclaimed.

"I'll say," Ned agreed. "I only wish I could have been with you and Di up there when you ran into those gangsters!"

"You could have substituted for me. Welcome to it,"

Diana said, shivering. "I don't enjoy Trixie's narrow escapes. You'll find out Miss Trask doesn't think much of them, either."

Diana was right. When Miss Trask learned of the latest episode she wanted to telephone Mr. Wheeler immediately.

"Daddy is in Washington," Honey reminded her. "And anyway—"

"Anyway, I can call Mr. Belden," Miss Trask went on. "I just don't want the responsibility of looking after all of you when these things keep happening. The very next time those men show up—and they will show up, you can depend on that—something tragic could happen."

"Not those guys," Mart said. "I think they're chicken."

"Why do you say that?"

"Because they've had half a dozen chances already to do real harm if they'd intended to. They've acted like one of those old cops-and-robbers comedies we see on late TV. They run for cover all the time. Take tonight, even. If they'd really wanted—"

"You'd have been as frightened as we were, Mart Belden," Trixie interrupted, "if you'd been way up there in that building all alone. I guess if you had my sore knee from being knocked down in the park, too, you wouldn't make fun of it."

"Trixie could have been badly injured when those men tripped her," Jim said soberly. "No, Mart, it won't do to write those men off as comics. On the other hand,

if they really are after the statue, we must find some
way of talking to them to find out why they want it.
If you'd call Dad, Miss Trask, or Trixie's dad, we'd all
have to go back home to Sleepyside right away."

"Oh, *please*, let's not have to do that," Barbara
begged. "We'd never have such a wonderful opportunity again to see and do things in New York. We're
thrilled to pieces about the whole business."

"I'm not," Miss Trask said emphatically. "Jim, what
was it you were going to say?"

"Let me say something first, please," Brian said
soberly. "We're inside the apartment now, and no one
is going to come here when we're all home. Tomorrow
Bob and Ned and Barbara want to see all the Lionel
trains in action. Bob has been looking forward to it.
It will be in daylight. Will you be willing to call off
getting in touch with Dad or Mr. Wheeler till after
then and, if those men don't show up again, forget it
till Bob and Barbara and Ned have finished their
visit to the city?"

"I certainly don't want to be a spoilsport," Miss
Trask said uncomfortably.

"Jeepers, thanks!" Trixie cried.

"You didn't let me finish what I started to say,
Trixie." Miss Trask was sober. "It's just this: I'll agree
to the daylight visit to the trains, but no more going
about at night!"

"Not even if you'd come with us?" Barbara asked.

"I can't do that, Barbara. At least, I don't think I
can, unless my sister gets much better—"

"Which we hope happens, no matter how it affects what we do," Honey said sincerely.

"I know that, dear. Let's just see what tomorrow brings. We'll take it from there. Is that all right?"

"Neat-o!" the twins chorused.

"People in New York City practically live in taxicabs, it seems to me," Barbara said the next day as she settled back into the seat next to Trixie.

"It would be a long walk from here to the Lionel showroom. We'll get there sooner this way."

"*If* we get there at all," Diana told Trixie, shivering as the driver went down a narrow street, with only inches separating him from the double-parked cars. He turned to the girls in the backseat. "Don't you kids ever try that!" he chuckled, then turned back to fight his way over potholes in the pavement and in and around cars and trucks. Finally, with a flourish, he drew up in front of the Lionel trains showroom.

"There you are, buddy," he told Jim in the seat next to him. "It'll be a dollar seventy. Never thought I'd make it, did you, little lady?" he asked Barbara as she hurried out of the cab.

"I honestly didn't," she told him.

Then she colored as he shouted with satisfaction, "I always do! Ride with me, and you won't have to mess around gawking at scenic railways in the park for a thrill."

Inside the showroom there was a maze of trains—

big, little, antique, diesel, electric. Cars for every conceivable use stood on tracks leading to every conceivable kind of terminal.

"Here are your hats," a smiling attendant told them as he met them at the door and fitted them out with blue-and-white-striped caps bearing the inscription LIONEL ENGINEER. The boys pocketed theirs, for they really were intended for little-boy heads. The girls jauntily pulled theirs on.

"Make yourselves at home," the guide told them. "Stay as long as you want. Go wherever you want. If you don't find the train you're looking for, let me know. We've got it someplace."

"I'm sure you have," Barbara said, bewildered. "I've never seen so many trains before in all my life. Even big ones. There's a railroad junction at Valley Park in Iowa near where we live. Ned and Bob and I and our gang have gone there to watch the engines turn around in the roundhouse, but, heavens, there must be a million trains here!"

"I still like the trains over at Reeds' better," Jim said, looking around him.

"Is that a boy you know?" Barbara asked, then blushed when the Bob-Whites laughed.

"I'm sorry," Jim said when he saw Barbara's embarrassment. "I mean the model railroad that belongs to Dr. Joe."

"Dr. Reed," Trixie explained. "He's just about the most important orthopedic surgeon in the whole city of New York."

"In the whole *world!*" Diana insisted. "He operated on my little brother's leg when he broke it in three places. It's as good as ever now. That's when we met Dr. Joe. I do wish you could see his trains. It's a wonder he isn't here today. Trains are his hobby, and he haunts this place whenever he can get a minute off. Today *is* the day most of the doctors take off each week, isn't it, Jim?"

"Right! I'll bet a penny we'll find him in one of these rooms before we go, probably buying some kind of equipment. He calls his railroad the 'B and J.'"

"It's for 'Bone and Joint,'" Trixie explained. "I wish we'd run into him. We're all just crazy about him. Everyone who knows him is—big, little, any age. His wife, Betty, is just as wonderful, and their children are honeys. There's Tex—he's about ten and the oldest —then Chris and Jeff, twins, about seven, and little Nancy, four."

"I suppose he built the railroad for the boys," Ned said.

"Heavens, no!" Trixie answered. "He's the owner, builder, chief dispatcher, chief engineer— Hey, there he is! Dr. Joe! Dr. Joe!"

A big, handsome, dark-haired man put down the transformer he was examining and hurried to the young people, both hands outstretched. "Your father told me you were all here in the city, Diana, but I never thought I'd run into you. Is one of your visitors a model railroad bug?"

"Bob is, I guess," Trixie said. "Dr. Joe, these are our

friends from Iowa—Barbara and Bob Hubbell, and Ned Schulz."

"I'm a railroad bug, all right," Bob acknowledged with a smile, "but I don't have a railroad."

"He has a collection of old trains he saved from when he was little," Barbara said. "Now he's adding other antique trains as he finds them."

"The Bob-Whites have just been telling us about your Bone and Joint Railroad, sir. That's a neat name for it," Ned said.

Mart grinned. "It's a neat railroad."

"Why don't you come home with me to our apartment and have a look at it?" Dr. Reed suggested cordially. "My wife and the kids would be delighted. Do you have time to fit it into your schedule?"

"Oh, Dr. Joe, you just know we were waiting here with our fingers crossed, just hoping you'd ask us. We're shameless, but, jeepers, it'd be terrific!" Trixie was overjoyed to think the Iowans would have a chance to see the B & J.

"Then come along with me. I've parked the station wagon down on Twenty-sixth. We can all crowd into it. Betty uses it to take twelve kids to school in her car pool. I'll take this transformer along and try it," he told the salesman.

The Reed apartment was huge. From the moment they went in the door, the visitors knew it was a house filled with love and fun. The boys and little Nancy rushed to meet their father and nearly smothered him with bear hugs. Then, almost immediately, they adopted the Iowans as their "best friends," to fit the classification already given to the Bob-Whites.

"Cokes, anyone?" Betty Reed asked. Without waiting for an answer, she brought in tall glasses with ice clinking. "Do you want to go into the railroad room now?" she asked with a smile.

"He had the room designed especially for his trains," Jim said as they followed their host. "Every single, solitary thing in this whole room Dr. Joe built himself —trains, scenery, towns, everything!"

"Now, now, not the transformers! Betty helped, too, and the kids, with the rest of it." Dr. Reed stood just inside the door, quite obviously delighted at the amazement on the Iowans' faces.

Before them, on a wide terrain raised about three feet from the floor, they saw the most elaborate model railroad system imaginable. There must have been at least three complete trains, passenger and freight. There were refrigerator cars, coal cars, automobile carriers, piggyback flatcars, cars carrying logs, tank cars, even rolling aquarium cars with live goldfish. There were coaches for passengers, dining cars, club cars luxuriously fitted with upholstered chairs, and, finally, saucy red cabooses to tag at the ends of the freight trains.

Dr. Joe went up into the control room a few feet above the tracks and set his trains in motion. The young people crowded around, cheering the little engines, watching them whiz over trestles high above water and snake through long tunnels.

They watched the vigorous diesel-electric engine pull loaded cars to a mining town halfway up a mountain, then roar back to a village on the plain below. They saw an apparatus on the mail car catch tiny mail sacks from extended poles. Over the tracks the tiny trains flew. Freights were switched aside for main-line passenger trains to pass. In a roundhouse, engines turned for repairs.

"It's magic!" Barbara cried as Dr. Joe finally threw the switch and the cars slowed and stopped.

"It's the greatest!" Bob rubbed the back of his neck. "I think my head turned completely around trying to see everything! I wonder if Tex and the others are ever allowed to go up in the control tower."

"Sure! Dad lets us help with everything," Tex answered.

"Only when he's here, though," one of the twins added.

"Climb up here and have a go at it, Bob." Dr. Joe surrendered the control. "Take it easy . . . that's it!"

Excitedly, Bob watched the cars obey his guiding hand. "I never saw anything like it! Gosh, one thing's true, Barb . . . I'm going to shelve the antique cars and start a real, live railroad system. Look at her go! It'd take a lifetime, though, to ever get an outfit like this going."

"I guess it would, Bob," Barbara admitted. "How do you make the scenery, for instance?"

"It's a breeze. Even Nancy can tell you how to do it. She made some of the trees up there on the hill,"

Dr. Joe said, pointing toward a cluster of tiny trees.

"Yeah, the crooked ones," Chris said with brotherly frankness.

"They're made from pieces of sponge, or sponge rubber, dyed and glued to balsa sticks," Tex said. "We make the tunnels out of paper soaked in water and mixed with paint sizing. It turns into papier-mâché, and we pile it on top of wire forms, then color it brown to mark the entrances and exits."

"You tell them, Jeff, how we make the mountains," Dr. Joe suggested.

"They're made of burlap covered with patching plaster—painted brown, of course."

"We make the grass out of pieces of Turkish toweling dyed and glued to the ground," Chris explained.

"The only thing Mom does is to feed the animals and clean up after them," Mrs. Reed said.

"That's the biggest part," Dr. Joe said, putting his arm around his wife and smiling.

"Speaking of eating—and *my* characters are always doing that—" Betty Reed said, "can't you all stay and have dinner with us? We'd love it."

"All this gang?" Trixie said, aghast. "Heavens, no! That would be sixteen people."

"What of it? We'll have a cookout on the terrace— hamburgers—and you can all help. Jim, Dan, Brian, Mart, you get the fire going, and the girls can help me rustle up some salad. Stay, won't you?"

"Do! Please do!" the Reed children begged.

"We'd love it, of course, if you really mean it,

wouldn't we?" Trixie turned to her crowd.

"If we can help, yes," Honey said, "and that means doing the dishes, too. What's the matter, Mart?"

"I just happened to remember. I'm afraid we'd better not stay. Bob and Barbara sort of wanted to see the video tape of the show. We'd like to see it, too."

"What is it?" Mrs. Reed asked. "Is it something on television? Can't we all watch it?"

"Gee, sure, if you want to," Bob said, a little embarrassed. "It's kind of dumb."

Trixie explained that the show Barbara and Bob had appeared on the day before had been video taped for showing later in the evening. When she told the children that Barbara and Bob played guitars and sang songs they themselves composed, the Reed twins, enchanted with the visiting *older* twins, insisted they all stay.

So Mrs. Reed thawed chopped meat from their big freezer, mixed it with bread crumbs soaked in milk to keep the patties juicy, seasoned them, and passed them on to the boys to cook. The charcoal grill was hot. Dr. Joe donned a tall white chef's hat, and he and Jim and Brian quickly browned the hamburgers.

The fragrance of meat cooking, the tangy salad dressing, muted sounds from the avenue below—all provided a magical setting for the visitors. Bob and Barbara sang as Tex strummed his ukulele. Dr. Joe and his wife added their voices, and even little Nancy chimed in with her childish treble.

Later, as the coals whitened and when they had

consumed the food like a swarm of locusts, the young people gathered paper plates and cups and carried them to the kitchen.

"Time for the broadcast!" the Reed twins sang out.

Dr. Joe wheeled the portable television set out to the terrace, and they all crowded around it to watch and listen.

A Mysterious Call • 14

I THINK I'D BETTER hurry inside and telephone Miss Trask before the program starts," Trixie said. "I don't know why I didn't think of it before. We promised her that today we wouldn't go anyplace after dark."

"Tell her I'll take you all home," Dr. Reed called after her.

"Joe loves to have an excuse to drive through the theater district at night," Mrs. Reed explained while Trixie made her call. "We never have enough time to *go* to a show."

"I have to stop at the hospital, anyway," Dr. Joe said. "Did you get Miss Trask, Trixie?"

"Yes, I did, and she said she wouldn't worry as long as we're with you. Jeepers, the show's starting!"

When "Old Man River" was sung, the children clapped, delighted. "He has a marvelous voice," Mrs. Reed said. "Why, there are Barbara and Bob now, right on the screen. Do you see them, Nancy?"

"Shhh!" Nancy warned. Then, when the twins had finished their song, she ran to Barbara and threw her arms around her. "It was pretty music. You looked so pretty—"

"Oh, look!" Trixie screamed and pointed. All the Bob-Whites jumped to their feet.

"Did you see them?" Trixie exclaimed. "Away in back when the camera was turned on the audience?"

"You couldn't miss them," Jim said soberly.

"That wasn't any coincidence, their being at the broadcast!" Trixie grabbed Honey's hand.

"Heavens, no!" Honey said. "Trixie, we sure bungled this job. We still haven't anything but the faintest idea of why they are following us."

"Is the whole thing a secret?" Dr. Joe asked.

Trixie's face sobered. "Oh, how rude of us! It isn't a secret at all, but it's a long story. It sure is a strange mystery, too."

"Then tell us," Tex cried. "Tell us, please!"

"If you do, begin with the Mexican woman at Kennedy Airport," Barbara said. "It all seems to fit together. It's the thrillingest thing!"

So Trixie told the story of the woman at the airport; her prophecy and the amazing way it seemed to be working out; the little Incan idol purchased at the antique shop; her accident in Central Park; the episode at Liberty Island; the men who hung around their apartment entrance; the strangers who searched the apartment; Trixie and Diana's experience at the Empire State Building—all the odd things that had happened since they had been in the city.

"We haven't seen those men all day," Trixie concluded, "so we thought that we could forget about them."

"If you'd looked at the prophecy again you'd have known what to expect," Diana said. "I remember it: 'Be not misled by evening's fun; a villain's work is never done.'"

"You're right, Di! Then just after that it says: 'Twin rails of steel, a trembling square, watch close, you'll see the guilty pair.'" Trixie was so excited she could hardly speak. "Doesn't that mean Dr. Joe's model railroad, and the 'trembling square' surely means the television screen!"

"Golly!" Tex said, awed. "Golly whiz! Aren't you scared to death now, Trixie?"

"No, I'm not. I'm just furious at myself because it all baffles me so."

Dr. Reed wore a deep frown. "This thing is serious, Trixie. Of course you've reported these things to the police. . . ."

"We have, but we've never had a good enough look at the men before to be able to describe them well." Trixie sighed. "The police say they can't do a thing till they have a definite idea of what the men look like."

"Of course you've reported it to your fathers." Dr.

Reed looked inquiringly at Jim, Diana, and Trixie.

"No, we haven't—" Trixie began.

"We haven't been in any *real* danger—" Honey continued.

Trixie interrupted. "Miss Trask is staying with us, and we begged her not to tell our families unless something really serious turned up. We didn't want to have to go right home without showing the rest of the city to Barb and Bob and Ned. Besides—"

"I know, Trixie, I know. You didn't want to have to stop in the middle of solving a mystery. Oh, Trixie!" Dr. Joe put his arm around Trixie's shoulder. "I have every respect in the world for Miss Trask, but serious things *have* happened. Maybe you haven't emphasized them enough when you've told them to Miss Trask. She's such a grand person she'd never want to spoil your good time here. I do honestly think that Mr. Wheeler should know, though."

Tex protested. "Oh, Daddy, Trixie and Honey have solved worse cases. I want to know the ending."

"Trixie's on the job, for sure," Mart said. "Her mind's busy on the mystery all the time. You know how she is. She's not afraid of anything. She'd just as soon walk right into a cage with a pair of lions—"

"Which isn't wise," Dr. Joe declared firmly. "Since Miss Trask is your chaperon, the one your family has put in charge of you, I'd never intrude. There's one thing sure now: When the police see the video tape of the television show, they'll have a good look at the men who've been following you. They won't have any further reason not to swing into action."

"That's right!" Trixie agreed.

"Shall I call them now and tell them about it?" Jim asked.

"I think that's a good idea. Go into my study and use the telephone."

"If everyone would just let Trixie and Honey handle the thing themselves, they'd soon find out who the men are," Tex said confidently.

"Thanks, Tex," Trixie said. "I guess I'd have to have some cooperation from the police to accomplish that. I haven't quite graduated to detective work in as big a place as New York City."

"Gosh, it'd be a breeze for you here, after all the thieves you've rounded up!" Tex's eyes were round with excitement.

Jim came back from the telephone. "Did you get the police?" Trixie asked eagerly.

"Yes. They said they'd have to arrange with the Celebrity Broadcasting Company to show the tape in the morning. They told us to forget it tonight, and someone would call for one or two of us tomorrow morning to go with them to see the rerun."

"At least that will be a beginning," Dr. Reed said, apparently more satisfied. "If I can help you in any way, just give me a ring. I still think Mr. Wheeler should know about it."

"We'll know more ourselves after the police see the rerun," Trixie said. "I can't see why that little idol could have stirred up all this trouble."

"Do you possibly have it with you? Could we *possibly* see it?" Tex asked. "Please, Trixie!"

"I did carry it in my purse, but Miss Trask thought I should let her take care of it. She has it now. She'll give it back to me tonight so I can show it to the police tomorrow. It's a harmless-looking little statue."

"Ugly enough to be Mephistopheles himself," Mart said. "About so big"—he measured with his hands—"and almost all head. Why Trixie wanted it in the first place I'll never know."

"I wonder myself," Trixie said to herself softly.

"There's one thing sure: The prophecy that Mexican woman made is mere coincidence," Mrs. Reed said.

"You're right, Betty. I'm glad to see some of the fortune-tellers ousted from the city." Dr. Reed's face grew stern. "You have no idea how much occultism and how many crazy beliefs I run into in trying to treat some of the families here in New York City."

"It's queer about the prophecy, though," Trixie insisted. "Meeting that poor, bewildered Mexican woman seems strange, too. I don't think she should have been sent away."

"I guess the police know what they're doing," Dan protested.

"Right!" Dr. Reed agreed. "They're of inestimable help to me in my work. They're right on the ball when a child is involved in an accident. I set the bones and try to heal bodies, but the police furnish all the facts that help the poor families collect damages. That's mighty important. Say, kids, how would you like to stop at the hospital with me on the way home to your apartment? There's a little girl there who'd be thrilled to pieces to meet the singing twins of television."

"You know how *I'd* like to do that!" Brian exclaimed. "It's the most marvelous hospital, Ned. Dr. Joe used to let me watch sometimes when he dressed Terry's leg . . . he's Di's brother. I sure wish the time would come when I'd be able to help crippled and hurt children the way Dr. Joe does. Terry never cried once when the cast came off. I know it hurt him."

"Terry's a soldier. Most children are. I sometimes wish grown-ups had half as much courage," Dr. Joe said. "As for you, Brian, you'll make a great surgeon one of these days. I can tell."

Brian's eyes shone. "Thank you, sir!"

After the Bob-Whites and their visitors had helped restore order to Mrs. Reed's patio and kitchen, they thanked her, waved good-bye to the children, went down in the elevator, and all crowded into the big Reed station wagon.

Dr. Reed guided the car slowly and skillfully through the hordes of screaming taxis and shining limousines carrying the theater crowd; past the blazing strips of multicolored neon lights in the theater district; past the food stands in open stalls—hot dogs, Coca-Cola, ice cream, red-hot chestnuts. Finally the big car moved away from the bright lights and picked up speed on the expressway. Bob leaned back with a sigh. "All those famous places . . . gosh!"

"The most important one is just ahead—over there

where you see the circle of lights along the driveway. It's Dr. Joe's hospital!" Brian's eyes were like stars.

"Jeepers, just look at the size of it!" Ned exclaimed. "I thought Mercy Hospital in Des Moines was big."

"It makes me sad to think of all the sick people there," Trixie said. "There are hundreds of hospitals in New York City, too, all full of sick people."

"It makes me glad . . . glad they have a place to go and people like Dr. Joe to make them well," Brian said.

Dr. Reed parked the station wagon, and the young people jumped out and followed him through the emergency entrance and into a shining white elevator which shot them to the children's floor. Everywhere nurses smiled and called greetings to Dr. Reed. When they saw all the young people, they smiled again.

"May we go into Evalinda's room?" he asked the gray-haired floor nurse. "All of us?"

"Do, please, Doctor," she answered. "She'll be so glad to have visitors. She hasn't had one all day."

When Dr. Reed stepped into the hospital room, a small face, with a halo of bristling pigtails, turned into one big smile that spread from ear to ear.

"Dr. Reed!" the girl cried. "I was so lonesome."

"You won't be lonesome long, Muggins," Dr. Joe said with a warm smile. "See all the friends I brought to call on you. This is Trixie. She's a girl detective. This is her partner, Honey, and their friends Barbara and Diana. This is Jim, Honey's brother, Brian and Mart, Trixie's brothers, and their friend, Dan Mangan.

The others are Bob, who is Barbara's twin brother, and their neighbor Ned. Barbara and Bob and Ned live in Iowa. Shake hands with everyone the way I taught you!"

Since Evalinda's arms and both legs were in traction, Trixie couldn't imagine how she'd ever manage to shake hands. The others, too, watched curiously.

"They don't believe you know how to shake hands. Show them, Muggins," Dr. Reed urged the shy little girl. She smiled at him, raised her head, and shook it from side to side. Little tinkly bells jingled a fairy greeting. Then, as she saw the puzzled faces on her visitors, her broad smile came back. "They're tied to my top pigtails! Dr. Reed brought the bells to me last week. Dr. Reed thinks of everything."

"Everything but a way to make you eat so you'll get big and strong," a white-capped nurse said as she placed a foaming glass of malted milk with a bent sipper near the little girl.

"If you drink it down to here"—Dr. Reed indicated a line near the bottom of the glass—"I'll take the last sip for you, and you know, Muggins, every time I drink or eat . . . hocus-pocus! A fairy puts a present in my pocket for you!"

The little girl sucked and swallowed, sucked and swallowed till the liquid slowly reached the mark. Then Dr. Joe took the glass and drank the rest. Evalinda's big eyes traveled from one of his coat pockets to the other. When the last drop had disappeared, he reached into his pocket and pulled out a small cloth Chinese doll. "Her name is 'Pretty Blossom.' The magic thing about her is that you'll never get lonesome as long as her head is on your pillow."

He tucked the small doll next to the little dark head on the pillow, then said, "Guess what, Muggins. Yesterday Bob and Barbara, the twins here, appeared on a talent show at Celebrity Broadcasting Studio. They sang folk songs on television."

"Oh, Dr. Reed," Evalinda cried. "You know that's what I want to do most of all in the world. If you'd close the door, I'm sure Nurse won't mind if they'd just sing one little song. Will you please?"

"We'd love to sing for you," Barbara answered. "We sing better with our guitars, but maybe you won't mind if we sing without accompaniment."

So they sang:

> "Swing low, sweet chariot,
>   Comin' for to carry me home.
>   Swing low, sweet chariot,
>   Comin' for to carry me home."

Evalinda's clear voice took up the melody as they went on:

> "I looked over Jordan, and what did I see
>   Comin' for to carry me home?
>   A band of angels comin' after me,
>   Comin' for to carry me home."

Barbara and Bob stilled their voices gradually, and the little girl's sweet voice rose in solo just before the song's end.

When the nurse opened the door to signal them that it was time to leave, the young people threw kisses back to the tiny, brave patient. Then they waited in a cheerful sun-room at the end of the hall while Dr. Reed made several other calls.

"It was a wonderful evening," Barbara said as the doctor let them out at the door of the apartment building. "We loved the chance to see the railroad and to meet your family, and Evalinda, too."

"My family and I enjoyed having you," Dr. Joe said. "You could tell that from the way the kids acted. As for Muggins, she'll be talking about you till her small arms and legs are sturdy and strong."

"That'll be the day, sir," Brian said, his voice filled with deep respect.

The doorman let them into the apartment building. He touched Trixie's arm as she passed. "There's a telephone call for you, miss," he said.

Mart, overhearing, suggested, "Can't you take it upstairs?"

"I guess I can't," Trixie answered. "Whoever it is may be calling from a pay station or long distance. They'd just have to call back again. Go on upstairs, everybody, and I'll be right up. It may be just a wrong number again, Mart."

"Yeah, it may be, but they asked for you. Come on, gang; let's see if Miss Trask caught the video tape show. She just might have noticed those guys in back."

Trixie went into the booth, took up the receiver, and said, "Hello? This is Trixie Belden."

A man's guttural voice answered.

"What did you say?" Trixie inquired. "Meet you where? Who are you?"

"You know who I am."

She could barely make out the reply.

"Are you—you're one of the men who've been following us all the time. Why didn't you tell us what you want?"

The caller ignored her question. "You got the statue?"

"Yes, I have it. . . . You say it belongs to a rich man in Peru? . . . Someone stole it? Well, I didn't steal it. I bought it."

The man muttered something in a foreign language. Then he said, "I give you thousand dollars for it."

Trixie could hardly believe what she was hearing. "A thousand dollars! Wow! I surely know where that much money would do a lot of good. You just come up here to our apartment tomorrow, and I'll hand over the statue."

"No!" The word was sharp. "Listen to me now. . . ." A torrent of words followed, and Trixie listened intently as the man gave instructions.

"I see. You belong to the secret police. Where did you say I should meet you? . . . By myself? I'm sorry. I surely couldn't go anyplace tonight by myself."

The flow of words began again. From time to time Trixie nodded.

"Tomorrow in broad daylight? That's different, but I still couldn't go anyplace by myself. Why do you want me to go alone? . . . What? . . . Is it *that* secret? Well. . . ."

There was a note of pleading in the voice at the other end.

"A restaurant? With lots of people in it? A table in the center of the room? . . . Heavens, a thousand dollars! . . . Well, I won't say I'll go, but give me the address. I'll have to think it over."

Jeepers, Trixie thought to herself as she slowly replaced the receiver, *that's something for me to think about! Secret police! He said I couldn't tell a soul. That means I can't even tell Honey. I would like to get rid of that statue. . . . A thousand-dollar reward! What will I tell the gang when they ask who called me? I guess I'll just have to say someone was calling about something I bought. Mart won't let me get away with that, I'm afraid.*

It was exactly what Trixie told Mart, for he was the first to ask. She was sure he never would have accepted what she answered, without smelling a rat, if they hadn't all been so busy telling Miss Trask about the wonderful evening.

That night Trixie tossed from side to side almost the whole night, her mind spinning from one decision to another.

Trixie's Secret Meeting · 15

THE EARLY MORNING SUN streamed through the window next to Trixie's bed and fell across her face. Startled, she awakened, thought a moment, then slipped quickly out of bed.

"I'm going to meet those men," she said to herself determinedly. "If I can only slip downstairs and out of doors before anyone else is up. I *can't* let anyone know where I'm going. There's no danger in it in broad daylight!"

As she hastily put on her clothes, she tried very hard to convince herself she was right. "I think it's worth taking a tiny little chance if I can get the thousand-dollar reward. When the Bob-Whites give the money to the fund for the station wagon for crippled children, they'll be all through scolding me."

As Trixie cautiously turned the knob of their bedroom door, Honey moved restlessly and sighed. "Oh, dear, she just mustn't wake up," Trixie thought and left the door slightly ajar to avoid the click it would make if she closed it. "Now, if I can get from here to the hall, I'll be all right. . . . Oh! There's Miss Trask's shower going! Well, what am I worrying about? She won't hear me when I open the door to the foyer. It's a good thing she left the little statue on my dressing table. She'll be glad to know, when I get back, that we don't have to go to the studio to show the police a rerun of the video tape. Everyone will be glad when I get rid of the statue, the mystery is solved, *and* I show them the thousand dollars! Oh, dear, I hope I can get there and back before anyone misses me!"

The taxi driver was an elderly man. He drove skillfully through the morning traffic, north on Broadway until he left the crowded district far behind. Then he speeded up.

"This isn't a very nice part of the city," Trixie thought. "It looks awfully dingy." She stared in pained astonishment at a man asleep on a doorstep. "Are you sure this is the address I gave you?" she asked the driver.

"*I'm* sure, miss, but are you?" he answered. He stopped at a dilapidated building with a crooked sign across the front, JAKE'S HAMBURGER PLACE. "This don't look like a high-school hangout to me. Is this the place?" The taxi driver frowned.

Trixie looked at the address on the slip of paper in her hand. "It's the same number they gave me. Is this a bad part of the city?"

"It ain't St. Patrick's Cathedral. What you goin' to do here, kid?"

"Meet some people."

"People you know?"

"Yes—well, sort of."

"That must be all right, then." The driver shrugged his shoulders. "Fare's a dollar sixty. Kids go to the craziest places nowadays."

"Is it dangerous around here?" Trixie was a little alarmed at what the driver had said.

"Depends on how you look at it. I've delivered some queer characters to this place. Makes me wonder if it's really hamburgers they sell here. Ain't never seen any police raidin' the place, though."

"Can you come back for me in half an hour?"

"Sorry, kid." The driver shook his head regretfully. "I can't promise that. I might be tied up. I'll give it a try. Tell you what: If I am tied up, I'll send someone back here to pick you up. Okay?"

"Okay, I hope." Trixie climbed out of the taxi and looked around cautiously.

There wasn't a soul on the street. Jake's Hamburger Place showed no sign of life. When Trixie tried the door, however, it opened easily. For a moment she didn't see anything, for the change from bright sunlight outside to half-darkness inside blinded her. Then, off in a corner next to the wall, she saw a single electric light bulb glowing dimly above a table where two men sat.

As Trixie entered the room, one of the men stood up. He was small and stocky. He had a livid scar across his forehead, down one eyelid, and well into his cheek.

From behind the counter on the other side of the room, a third man spoke. "Coffee, miss?"

"No, thank you. I must hurry back home for my breakfast. You *are* the man who telephoned to me, aren't you?" she asked the scar-faced man at the table.

"I am. Come over here to the table. My friend's here. We talk business."

Trixie accepted the chair he offered against the wall next to his seated friend. When she sat down, she was hemmed in between the two men.

"Now, sister," said the man with the scar, "we talk. The idol you got belongs to Don Alfonso Alfredo. We come from his hacienda in Peru. It's a idol been in the family a thousand years. Somebody steal it, bring it to this country. He wants it back."

"He's gonna get it back!" the other man said. Tall, olive-skinned, his face creased with wrinkles, he was more hideous-looking than Scarface. He moved closer to Trixie menacingly. She felt suffocated . . . frightened . . . more terrified than she ever had been in her life.

"I'm prepared to return it," she said in a trembling voice. "You told me you would pay me a thousand dollars for its return. I only came here because I want to give that thousand dollars to a fund in Sleepyside—

the fund to buy a station wagon to take crippled children to school."

"Well, now, isn't that a charitable thing to do?" the man over at the counter sneered.

Startled, Trixie looked across the room to the third man. "Why, you—you're the man at the United Nations —and at the Museum of Natural History! There *are* three of you!"

"Exactly! So you can count, can't you?" the man answered Trixie in a mocking voice. "If you had been a clever girl, you'd have handed the statue over to me in the first place. It would have saved you a lot of trouble. If *I* had been clever, I'd have taken it from you by force at the gift shop in the United Nations."

"You shoulda got rubbed out for missin' it, Pedro. Wipe that smile off your face!" The scar-faced man scowled.

"Watch your language, Blinky!" Pedro glared at the scar-faced man. "Can I help laughing when I think of you and Big Tony in the welfare racket? A thousand dollars for crippled children!"

Big Tony stood up. "That's enough outta you! I got business to take care of. Come on, sister, hand over the idol! We ain't got all day to wait!"

"Softly there, Tony. Treat the young lady gentle!" Blinky said with a cruel smile. "I got her purse, see? I'll hand it over to ya in justa—say, kid, if you double-crossed us. . . ."

He shook the contents of Trixie's purse onto the table. Her compact rolled to the floor. Her lipstick followed. Blinky opened her coin purse. He handed the bills to Big Tony.

"Don't you dare touch my belongings!" Trixie cried, her eyes blazing. "Where is the reward you promised me?"

"Yes. Yes. I call that a good question, now," Pedro called from across the room. "Where is the young lady's thousand dollars? Take it from your bankroll, Blinky. Give it to her!" Pedro laughed loudly again, at his own joke.

Big Tony picked up Trixie's purse and threw it with terrific force across the room. It struck Pedro right in the face, blinding him for a moment. Then he brushed his hand across his eyes, vaulted the counter, and lunged toward the table. In a flash Big Tony whipped out his gun. He aimed it at Pedro's chest, ordering him back to his place behind the counter. Cursing, Pedro obeyed.

"Now, sister, where's the idol?" Tony asked tersely as he returned his gun to its holster.

For some reason she would never be able to understand, Trixie had concealed the small idol deep in the pocket of her skirt. Terrified, she reached to get it. In a second Big Tony whipped out his gun again and turned it on her. "One kid like you less in the world ain't gonna bother me one bit," he sneered. "Hand it over, kid."

Almost fainting, Trixie tried to answer. She tried to reach into her pocket. Her hands were paralyzed. Her voice failed. *Why did I ever come here?* she thought desperately. *I'll be killed, and no one will ever know what happened to me.*

"Slow down, Tony!" Blinky yelled. "Can't ya see the kid's too scared to talk? The idol ain't in her purse. We gotta find out where it is. Don't let that gun go off, Tony. Remember what happened when ya knocked off that guy at the bank? We lost twenty grand, that's all. If we was caught, we'd 'a' got the chair. Don't scare the kid before we get the idol. He ain't gonna harm you none, kid."

"Oh, ain't I?" Big Tony pushed the gun right up against Trixie's side. Everything began to swim around her. *I can't faint,* she thought and shook her head vigorously. "If—you'll—just—wait—a—second—" she said, her voice hardly audible.

"Speak up!" Big Tony prodded her in the side with his gun. "You're takin' forever! I ain't a patient man. This gun might go off. Just keep your hands on the table!"

"Then—how—can—I—?"

"Come across, kid, or else. . . ."

He's going to kill me! "Jim! Jim! Jim!" Trixie's voice rose to a scream.

Across the room, Pedro signaled frantically toward the street, his hand held high, pointing. "Cut it, Blinky, Tony—cops! Didn't you see me trying to warn you?" He disappeared below the counter.

A burly policeman burst through the door, followed by Jim, Dan, Brian, Mart, Bob, and Ned! Before they could reach the corner, Blinky and Big Tony had lifted a trapdoor back of the table and had disappeared down the opening.

Trixie huddled at the table alone. She was hardly aware of Jim and Mart lifting her to her feet.

"Get her out of here into the air!" Brian commanded, and the others stepped back out of the way. Outside, Brian rubbed his sister's hands vigorously while Jim gently stroked her head, his forehead wrinkled in deep concern. Slowly, very slowly, the color came back into her face and lips. Big tears filled her eyes.

"Did you get—those men? Blinky, Pedro—Big Tony? Big Tony was going to shoot me!" A shudder ran through Trixie's body. "Did you get them?" she repeated as the policeman pushed his way toward her.

"Blinky, you said? Big Tony? Pedro?" The policeman turned to Dan. "It's a miracle she's alive. Do you know who they are?"

Dan shook his head. "Pretty bad actors, I guess. I do know this place is a hideout for gangsters."

"You said it, boy." The policeman nodded and went on, "Those men are three of the cleverest, most ruthless jewel thieves in the world. They've given us the slip now—through that trapdoor, up a ladder, over rooftops. There are a dozen escape routes in a radius of half a block, some of them underground. The whole place is a rat run."

"I know," Dan said. "Why you ever came here, Trixie. . . ."

Trixie tried to answer. Her voice choked. She was the sorriest girl in the whole world. It was a dreadful thing she had done, she thought, dreadful not only because of her own risk, but also because she had imperiled the lives of those she loved. Big Tony could have blazed his gun at *them* before he disappeared.

"How did you find me?" she asked weakly.

"It was Dan," Mart answered.

"Not me entirely," Dan said. "If it hadn't been for the doorman—"

"I think we should get Trixie home," Brian interrupted. "This crowd is getting bigger all the time. She needs to rest. Her nerves are shot. Let's get her out of this place."

"Right you are, Brian," Jim said.

A taxi had been edging its way along the curb. It stopped at Jim's signal. The driver got out and opened the door. "I drove the kid here," he announced when he saw Trixie.

"He did," Trixie told her friends. "He tried to keep me from stopping here."

"Good for you, Pete!" the policeman said. He held the crowd back while the young people got into the taxicab. "Get her out of here now, driver. Stand back, all of you. Stand back!"

When they had driven a little way up the street, Jim asked the driver to stop at a drugstore so he could make a phone call. "To Miss Trask," he explained. "I told her I'd call."

Poor Trixie, revived a little now, dreaded to go back to the apartment, where she'd have to explain what she had done.

"Dad answered the phone," Jim reported when he returned. "Miss Trask had called him at his office."

Now Trixie was really worried.

At the apartment they found Honey, Diana, and Barbara in tears. Miss Trask's face was white, Mr. Wheeler's stern.

"I did an awful thing . . ." Trixie began.

"Oh, Trixie, why . . . why . . . why?" Honey asked, her eyes red with weeping. "We were sure you had been murdered. When Dan told us about that awful place—"

"Dan told you about what?" Trixie asked.

"Sit down in this big chair, Trixie," Miss Trask told her quietly, giving Trixie a glass of hot milk. "Try to relax. Then we'll tell you about Dan."

"Yes, do," Mr. Wheeler said, and he put a pillow at Trixie's back.

"Don't *anyone* be kind to me!" Trixie protested. "Instead, you should think of the worst words in the world to say to me. They said they'd pay me a thousand dollars if I'd turn that idol over to them!"

"When did anyone say that to you?" Honey asked. "We've been with you everyplace you've gone."

"It was that telephone call last night!" Mart said triumphantly. "Wasn't it, Trixie?"

"Yes, it was," Trixie admitted reluctantly. "It was Blinky. He told me I had to go alone. He said I'd be in no danger, that he was a member of the secret police, and that he'd meet me in a restaurant filled with people in broad daylight."

179

"But we promised we'd never go anyplace by ourselves," Diana reminded her. Her face was tear-stained.

"I forgot about that part of it," Trixie said truthfully. "I was so anxious to get that thousand-dollar reward. How was I to know it would be a dingy old place in a horrible neighborhood?"

"You could have confided in one of us," Mart said sternly.

"In me, at least," Honey added tearfully.

"Not one of you would have let me go!"

"You never spoke a truer word," Mart answered. "For someone smart, you sure can be—"

"Dumb. I know it, Mart." Trixie's shoulders slumped. "It was dumb of me to think I could outsmart big city crooks. I do still have the little idol, though. They didn't get that away from me. They told me it belongs to a nobleman in Peru, that it was stolen from him. We don't even know if that's true."

"I'll take the idol now," Mr. Wheeler said firmly. "If it's worth a thousand-dollar reward to a couple of thieves, it has too much value for a young girl to be carrying around. How do you feel now, Trixie?"

"I feel all right physically, if that's what you mean. But I sure do feel awful otherwise. I'm trying not to think what Moms and Dad will say when they find out what I did."

"Wait till you're back home safely before we tell about this part of your New York stay," Mr. Wheeler said wisely.

"Oh, *will* you do that? I'll be grateful to you all the rest of my life."

"I'll not expect that." Mr. Wheeler smiled. "The reason I'm willing to wait to tell them is that I'll keep the idol with me. I'll be right with you, too, everywhere you go in the evening. I'm sure Trixie won't run off to any wild place again. I'll keep in close touch with the police; you can depend on that."

"Dad, you're the greatest!" Jim exclaimed. "I think Trixie's had enough punishment for now. You are feeling better, aren't you, Trixie? Are you sure you're all right?"

"I'm sure. Even if I don't deserve to be, I am." Trixie smiled wanly. "What I don't understand is how anyone knew where to find me. I thought it was a miracle when your call came through the door of that horrible place. What did you mean about Dan and the doorman?"

"Let Dan tell it," Honey suggested. "We sure are lucky to have him for a Bob-White member."

"It was one time my knowledge of the shady part of this town paid off," Dan said. "When you didn't come back for such a long time, we started to worry. First we thought you'd been in a street accident. Then we went downstairs and asked Mr. Hawkins, the doorman, if you had said anything when you left."

"When he told us you hadn't, we really were scared," Diana said.

"Then he remembered you'd asked him for a piece of paper to copy something you'd written on the phone book in the booth," Diana went on. "Have you ever looked inside the cover of a telephone book in a public booth? Everyone writes something there—telephone numbers, addresses. . . ."

"How could you tell what *I'd* written? It was only the number of the place where they told me to meet them."

"I haven't tutored you in math for nothing," Jim said. "I recognized the funny figure four you always make. That was enough for Dan. He knew exactly where you'd gone, and he knew you'd be sure to run into danger."

"It was near the neighborhood where I lived after my mother died," Dan put in. "I know every inch of it, and it's bad. The joint where you went is a place a 'fence' operates. A fence disposes of stuff thieves take to him."

Dan paced up and down the room nervously. "So then we called the police, and they came right away. That ride in the squad car was the longest ride I ever took in my life."

"It was for me, too," Jim declared. "Trixie, I'll never forget how I felt when we found you!"

Trixie held Jim's hand tightly. With her other hand she caught Dan's hand. For a long time she didn't speak.

"Three of them!" she finally said. "That was what was so puzzling and why we were never able to tell the police exactly what they looked like. Big Tony was the tall one of the pair who followed us. Pedro was the one who pretended to be a Peruvian. He talked to us at the United Nations."

"And at the Museum of Natural History!" Honey added. "Trixie, we never trusted him. And what about the other man, the one with the scar across his eye?"

"Blinky, yes." Trixie hid her face. "He's so horrible-looking with his big bald head and squinting eye—"

" 'Great headed man, with blinking eye'!" Mart cried. "It's Blinky to a T!"

Trixie jumped from her chair. "It is! It is! Where's my purse? That policeman gathered up my things from the floor and gave me my purse. Where is it? Oh, yes . . . here's the prophecy. What else did that Mexican woman say after the line about the TV studio? Here it is:

> "A lonesome journey, gleaming gun,
> Foolish girl, what have you done?

" 'Foolish girl,' " Trixie repeated sadly. "That's me, all right!"

Lost Forever · 16

Since the Iowans had to leave the next afternoon, Trixie insisted she was well enough to carry out their original plan for dinner on the plaza at Rockefeller Center that evening. Her experience with the men that morning had left her unnerved, though. Only one good thing emerged from it: The police knew now exactly who the men were who had been pursuing Trixie. They still did not know why. Mr. Wheeler had promised to take the small Incan idol to the police the next day, after the visitors left, so they might try to discover its attraction for the thieves.

The telephone rang. Mr. Wheeler answered it.

"Yes, Joe. Say, thanks for the way you put all these kids back on the right track. If your advice had only been taken. . . . You should have been around here this morning. Miss Trask and I went through several bad hours. Some of the young people did, too. Sure, you might know it was Trixie. Hold on; I'll let her tell all about it. It's Dr. Reed, Trixie . . . Trixie, where are you?"

"As soon as she heard you say 'Joe' she beat it to her room, sir," Mart said. "I don't wonder that she doesn't want to talk to him. He told us we might get into trouble, and she's ashamed to tell him she went off by herself. Let me talk to him. I'll tell him, if you don't want to."

"No, thanks, Mart." Mr. Wheeler smiled. "I'll tell him. Your version might be too vivid. Trixie has learned her lesson."

"Maybe she has *this* time," Miss Trask said doubtfully. "We always think so till something else happens."

So Mr. Wheeler told Dr. Reed about the events of the morning. He hadn't finished talking when Trixie came back into the room and asked to say something. Honey's father handed her the receiver.

"Dr. Joe, I'm *so* ashamed. I know it was a crazy thing to do, especially after what you said to us. Now those men have disappeared completely. There were three of them, instead of two. The police didn't have to look at the video tape after all. Blinky, Big Tony, and Pedro are well known to them. They think they're the slipperiest crooks they've ever encountered. Please don't tell Tex what I did. He thinks I'm a real detective. I'm going to be, too, one of these days. Next time

185

I won't be fooled so easily. Dr. Joe, are you still my friend?"

"Did he say he was your friend?" Diana asked after Trixie had put down the receiver. "Don't answer. I know he did. Dr. Joe seems to understand everything."

"He does, doesn't he?" Trixie answered thoughtfully. "He told me not to be so impatient to get started on a career. He's right, I know. I don't suppose we'll ever find out the real truth about my Incan statue. We've seen the last of those men, anyway. Or have we? Honey, if you ever catch a glimpse of Blinky— you couldn't miss him in a crowd—you tell me right away."

"There you go again!" Mart sighed.

"See here"—Mr. Wheeler's voice was very serious— "if *anyone* ever catches sight of any of those men, we want to know it. Only don't bother to tell Trixie first; just—"

"Call a cop!" Dan interrupted.

"Right!" Mr. Wheeler said. "Do it immediately. Now that they know the police are onto them, they just might try to make a last desperate move. Let's be alert constantly. Let's make the rest of the time count, too, before Barbara and Bob and Ned must leave. I'm going to stay right with you till we see the Iowans on the plane."

"Don't forget, Daddy," Honey reminded him, "that the plane from Orly Airport in Paris gets in not long before the Maine plane leaves. We told Sally, Billy, and Bob Wellington we'd meet them when they

186

arrived. They live near us in Westchester County," Honey explained to the Iowans, "only we never met them till we went to Di's uncle's ranch in Arizona. They've been traveling in Europe. Do you think you'd like to go with us to meet them?"

"And see a plane arriving from Paris?" Barbara asked enthusiastically. "I'd love to go."

"Someday you'll be taking a plane to Paris, when you and Bob are famous musicians," Trixie told the twins. "Even if you stick to your intention of teaching, you'll both be famous teachers!"

While Trixie, at Miss Trask's insistence, rested, Bob and Barbara and Ned packed everything except the clothes they needed to wear for dinner that night and on the plane to Maine the next day.

That night at Rockefeller Center, the plaza was a blaze of flowers, lights, fountains, and music. Everywhere people milled and crowded—some of them just walking down the concourse, many of them seeking seats in the open-air restaurant.

"We'll be lucky if we ever get a table in all this mob," Mart said, looking around him at the crowd.

"Daddy reserved one before we left the apartment," Honey said. "They're arranging it right now."

Busy busboys pushed smaller tables together to make room for the party of twelve, wedging the big table in close to other diners. The Bob-Whites apologized for crowding other guests.

Across from them, against the wall, the statue of

Prometheus stood out, two figures on either side, a boy and a girl. A lighted fountain played around them. Barbara could hardly take her eyes from it. "Everything in New York is the most!" she sighed.

"Even Blinky, Big Tony, and Pedro?" Mart teased.

Trixie shivered. "Let's not talk about them. I'm still ashamed. I'm ashamed, too, to think that Honey and I couldn't solve the mystery."

"You didn't give Honey much chance, Trix," Mart reminded her gently.

Honey went immediately to Trixie's defense. "I knew about all of it except the visit to that hamburger place. Trixie would have let me go there with her, too, except that Blinky told her she wouldn't get the thousand dollars unless she went alone."

"She didn't get it anyway, did she?" Mart was still critical.

"Not yet, but I seem to remember that the prophecy said she'll get a fortune. Did anyone read the next part of that verse?"

"I guess not, Honey," Brian said, speaking for the rest. "We were in too much of a stir about Trixie."

"That's what makes me so angry with myself, to think I was so dumb—" Trixie couldn't finish.

"Now, now, Trixie," Mr. Wheeler counseled, "let's forget it and all have a good time. Let the police take it from now on. I'm glad I have the idol now, instead of Trixie's carrying it around."

He reached into his pocket and brought it out. Suddenly someone passing jostled his arm. The statue fell to the ground. Frantic, he bent to retrieve it, then came up red-faced. "Who grabbed it from me?" He glared at Dan, next to him. "Was it you . . . for a joke?"

"What do you mean?" Dan looked bewildered. "I don't have it. When I bent over after it fell, I saw you pick it up. At least an arm—holy cow! Does *anyone* have it?"

In a second they were all down on the stone floor hunting about.

"I saw an arm reach for it," Mr. Wheeler insisted. "I felt someone push me. Where *is* the blasted statue?"

Neighboring diners and passersby—men, women, and children—most of them not even realizing what they were after, went down on their knees to help. The maître d'hôtel, quickly summoned, didn't like the commotion and said so.

"Ladies and gentlemen . . . " he began, then softened his voice as Mr. Wheeler pressed a bill into his hand. "Is there something I can do to help?"

"Not a thing!" Mr. Wheeler said tersely. "Trixie, come with me to telephone to the lieutenant at the police station. Jim, tell them to hold back my order, please. We'll be back in a minute."

"Please tell them to hold mine back, too," Trixie whispered to Jim.

"It was Blinky, of course," Trixie told Mr. Wheeler sadly. "It's fantastic the way he's appeared and disappeared."

"Like a greased monkey," Mr. Wheeler agreed. "No

one could ever believe it. He's so short he can slide in and out of a crowd like a snake. It finally paid off, didn't it, Trixie? Blinky and his pals have the statue now. I doubt if even the police will ever get it back."

"Don't say that! Honey and I *will* get it back, if we have to hunt it down the rest of our lives!"

"I don't think you'd be that foolish. If it's gone, it's gone. We might just as well accept it."

"It makes me furious." Trixie frowned fiercely. "We've never lost a case before. If I hadn't muffed this one! I can't bear not knowing why they wanted that statue. Now it's gone. Jeepers, Mr. Wheeler, I've just got to find out—"

"Here's the telephone. I'll call the police. I know the number. I should know it by this time. Calm down, Trixie. We're doing the only thing I know to try to get your statue back."

When they rejoined the group at the table, everyone tried to talk at once.

"I just made the report to the police. Trixie will tell you about it," Mr. Wheeler said.

"Hurry up!" Honey begged. "Were they excited when you told them the latest?"

"You bet they were!" Trixie's eyes shone. "There are some representatives of the Peruvian police here on the trail of *international* jewel thieves. They're sure Blinky, Big Tony, and Pedro are the ringleaders!"

"Gee! That's neat!" Bob exclaimed, all ears. "What's going to be the next move?"

"That's up to the police," Mr. Wheeler said.

"I guess it is," Trixie agreed. "The whole thing is queer, though."

"Of course it's queer, but do you mean something in particular? As if I didn't already know you do, without asking. You always mean something in particular when you use that tone of voice. What gives?" Mart asked curiously.

"I think I know what Trixie is thinking about," Honey said thoughtfully. "It's that prophecy again, isn't it?"

"Yes." Trixie hunted for the paper, found it, and spread it on the table. "It says here—"

"Read it out loud," Bob begged. "From the first. Maybe it'll give us a lead on what's going to happen next."

"I won't have time before they bring our food. I hope this works out before you have to leave."

"At least read the next few lines—the ones after 'foolish girl.'"

"That's me, Bob. Well, here it is. . . . Jeepers! Listen!

> "Great-headed man does prostrate lie,
> A bright stone in his blinking eye.

"Heavens, what do you think of that? I thought 'great-headed man' meant that Irish driver in the park at first. Then I thought it meant Blinky. But he doesn't 'prostrate lie.' At least, if he does I certainly don't know about it."

Honey jumped to her feet, so excited she could

191

hardly speak. "It's the statue! Its blinking eye must have hidden a jewel!"

"It didn't have a blinking eye. I looked over every inch of it—unless—jeepers, Honey, its eyes were enamel. I'd never call them 'blinking.' We never did look at the statue in the bright light, though. Maybe there was a crack in the enamel!"

"Before we get too carried away with that Mexican woman's words—" Miss Trask began.

"I know what you're going to say," Trixie interrupted. "But the prophecy has been right so far, hasn't it?"

"A person can twist words to get almost any meaning out of them he wants," Miss Trask said quietly. "Right now you're endowing that little idol with qualities no one ever noticed before."

"Miss Trask is dead right," Mr. Wheeler said. "Suppose we eat dinner. Let's descend from fancy to fact, before everything gets cold. We'll just let the law take its course."

"But they're so poky," Trixie said impatiently.

"What's so urgent about it?" Mart asked. "I'm with Miss Trask part of the way. There's a lot of gobbledygook in that so-called prophecy. What about toward the end: 'silver wings' and 'river's bend'?"

"That may mean we'll have to wait till we get back to Sleepyside to find out what happened to the statue," Trixie pointed out.

"Oh, I hope not!" Barbara cried. "We've just got to know how it all turns out."

"We may never know," Mr. Wheeler said realistically. "The police aren't successful in solving all the cases they undertake."

"Trixie is!" Honey insisted.

"With your help, Honey, and the help of all the Bob-Whites. I think we're going to know more about this soon. I just feel it in my bones!" Trixie smiled confidently.

"We'll all gather up our *leg* bones and amble back to the apartment, if you've finished your dinners." Mr. Wheeler smiled and called for the check.

"It's wonderful!" Barbara sighed. "This wonderful café, the wonderful fountain with its wonderful lights, and all the wonderful excitement about Blinky. It's all been—well, just—"

"Wonderful," Bob supplied. "So is your vocabulary, Barb." He smiled affectionately at his twin.

The Big Search • 17

DR. JOE was just leaving when Trixie and her group stopped in front of the apartment building. "I wanted to get the latest lowdown on the Belden-Wheeler case," he told them with a grin. "I don't dare to go home without a report for Tex and the twins."

"Come upstairs, and we'll give it to you," Mr. Wheeler invited. "It'll curl your hair, as Mart says."

Dr. Joe laughed. "I'm afraid I'd find that a major catastrophe. Did something interesting happen? I smell excitement in the air."

In the apartment, they told Dr. Joe about the loss of the idol. When Trixie's fancy started to roam, Mart held her to the bare facts. Dr. Joe listened intently to every word.

"I'm glad of one thing," he told Honey's father, "and that is that you've been herding this gang lately. That business of Trixie at the hamburger place still makes my blood run cold. What do you suppose is going to happen next?"

"Your guess is as good as mine, Joe. Say, there's the telephone. It may be the police calling."

Trixie was on her feet immediately. "I'll get it," she said.

They listened. "Hello." They saw Trixie's face redden, and it was easy to see that she was very angry.

"The police must be blaming Trixie for something," Honey said with concern.

Mart agreed. "Someone's mad at someone, for sure."

"Now you just listen to me a minute!" Trixie stamped her foot. "You say I've double-crossed you. That makes me laugh. You stole that statue right out from under our feet tonight— Stop shouting! I can't understand a word you say. The *diamond?*" Trixie turned to her listeners and held her finger to her lips to caution them to silence.

"Diamond!" Bob shouted. "Holy cow!"

"Why don't you and the others come to our apartment and discuss the matter with us?" Trixie continued. "I want to know who *really* owns the stone. It can't be very large. . . . What did you say? . . . What do I call large?"

"Bigger than a bread box!" Mart shouted.

"Be quiet, please," Mr. Wheeler warned. "Shall I talk to the man, Trixie?"

She shook her head vigorously, listened some more, then replaced the receiver.

"Jeepers!" Trixie looked dazed. "That's what the idol had inside his head—a big diamond! His head must have been split open when it hit the stone floor, and the stone dropped out. Let's call the police right away and tell them the latest."

"We'd better call the café, too. They were just closing when we left, though. The diamond is probably still on the floor there," Mr. Wheeler said.

Jim shook his head. "One of the dozens of people who were crawling around helping us try to find the statue probably found the diamond and pocketed it."

"I guess you may as well kiss it good-bye, Trix," Mart said.

"I certainly will not, Mart Belden." Trixie was almost shouting. "Blinky just said that stone is worth ten thousand dollars! Let's call the police now, then go back over to that restaurant and hunt again."

"It will be too late now, I'm afraid," Dr. Joe said sadly. "The floor will have been swept and the trash deposited with the tons of waste ready to be picked up in the morning. The cleaners move in fast as soon as the crowd leaves."

Trixie snapped her fingers. "I just thought of something! It may not be too late to search the sweepings from the café. I know I've read someplace that all the big office buildings save the accumulation of trash from each floor for a day before they burn it!"

"You're absolutely right. How smart of you, Trixie!" Mr. Wheeler exclaimed. "Why didn't I remember that? It's to keep valuable papers from being burned."

"*And* valuable diamonds from disappearing," Trixie said, her face one big smile. "What do I do next?"

"That's for the police to say." Mr. Wheeler quickly dialed the familiar number.

"If I'm going to see any of my patients at the hospital, I'd better be going," Dr. Joe said regretfully. "I guess I'll have to wait till morning for the next chapter. Say, I almost forgot to tell you all how grateful little Evalinda was for the stuffed rabbit you sent her. She sleeps with its nose right next to her face. Trixie, after all you've gone through, I surely hope you find that stone."

"It's a mystery to me how he could leave without knowing what the police say," Barbara said, her eyes bright with excitement. The Bob-Whites and their friends waited expectantly while Mr. Wheeler talked to the police. "I won't sleep a wink tonight, I know. Gosh, I *hope* the case is solved before we leave on the plane tomorrow. What did the police tell you?" she asked Mr. Wheeler as soon as he put down the telephone receiver.

"I had to wait while the officer called the head of the Peruvian police delegation," Mr. Wheeler reported. "Apparently, Trixie, that diamond is the key to the whole jewel robbery. There is a record of a shipment of twelve of those little wooden statues, all of them

197

assigned to that antique dealer where you bought yours. In them the thieves concealed diamonds that had formed a necklace stolen from an idol in a temple deep in the jungle in South America. One of the stones, a perfect blue-white one weighing about ten carats, was the center one in the necklace. The Peruvian police are pretty sure that is the one that was in the idol you bought, Trixie, because Blinky and Big Tony and Pedro have been giving you such a hard time. The police are sure you've put them on the trail of the other idols. They have that so-called antique dealer in custody."

Trixie's big blue eyes grew rounder. "What did they say is the next move? Did you tell them the diamond may be in the trash at that building?"

"I did," Mr. Wheeler reported. "Didn't you hear me? The officer told me we can't do a thing till morning. Besides, the crooks just could come back and step right into a trap. He'll ask then to have a search made. He said he'd try to get in touch with the custodian and see if the trash from the lower level has been added to the rest. Obviously it will make the search much easier if it hasn't."

"Then we have to sit on our hands till morning?" Trixie's face fell as Mr. Wheeler nodded.

"We'd better get a game of canasta or twenty questions going, then," Jim said quickly. "There'll be no sleep tonight for any of us."

"We can watch the late, late show," Mart said cheerfully.

198

"I think that's ridiculous, staying up all night. It will probably be almost noon before the police can possibly make any kind of a report. I'm going to bed." Mr. Wheeler picked up his hat and opened the door to go to the boys' apartment across the hall. "There isn't one single thing anyone can do till noon."

"I think I'll try to control my curiosity till then, too," Miss Trask said and bade everyone good night.

"I know what I'm going to do," Trixie announced determinedly. "At daylight I'm going back to the plaza and watch them sort the trash. Jim will go with me, won't you?"

"Of course," Jim said. "So will the rest of the gang, I know."

"You bet!" Ned agreed. "Let's get out the canasta cards. Two cents says the girls will fall asleep over the game. Barbara and Di are yawning right now."

"Not me!" Trixie said briskly. "Will you shuffle the cards, please, Jim?"

When the first light of dawn crept into the living room, Trixie, Jim, Dan, and Ned were the only ones awake. The rest were sound asleep in their chairs or on the sofa. Someone had turned off the television.

"We can go now," Trixie said. "We'll have to wake the rest, though. They'd never forgive us if we went without them."

"Barb and Bob wouldn't, for sure," Ned declared and nudged the twins to arouse them.

"Dad and Miss Trask will know we just couldn't

possibly wait any longer, since Bob and Barb and Ned have to leave this afternoon," Jim said. "I don't think they'll mind. It'll be daylight, and we'll all be together. I'll leave a note for them; then we'll get breakfast somewhere at the plaza."

No elevator was running in the apartment building, so they rushed down the ten flights of stairs to the street, too excited to be quiet.

Out on the street, the early morning traffic honked, banged, and whistled. An amazing number of people were hurrying to work. Trixie and her friends hurried even faster.

When they reached the plaza, it was deserted. They went to every entrance. All were locked. Lights shone here and there inside, but when Trixie and Jim peeked through the windows, they couldn't see anyone moving about.

Suddenly, out of nowhere, huge trucks backed up on the very low level of the building. Men in denims clambered out. Great doors swung open. The denim-clad men hurried through. Quick as a flash Trixie was after them, Jim right behind her.

"Hey, kids, where do you think you're going?" one of the truckmen called.

"Beat it!" a stocky maintenance man in front of the door shouted, barring the way.

"We had dinner here last night, out on the open terrace—" Trixie began.

"Yeah? So what?" the stocky man asked sarcastically.

"I lost a very valuable jewel. Haven't the police called about it?"

"At five o'clock in the mornin'? Are you kiddin'? Say, Mac," he called to someone inside the building, "seen anything of a diamond tiara?" He laughed and slapped his sides. "Watch out there, kids!" he called to the rest of the group who were trying to push their way inside. "Keep out of here, or I'll call a cop."

"But, don't you see, that's exactly what we want you to do!" Trixie insisted. "The police want to search the sweepings from the restaurant before all the trash gets mixed up together."

"Whyn't you say so?" the man asked. "Hey, Mac, you'd better talk to this kid. Maybe there's somethin' in what she's sayin'. Keep back there, the rest of you. Just you two," he told Trixie and Jim. "Wait outside, the rest of you. Hey, look. Here comes a cop now, Mac."

Mac and the policeman were soon in deep conversation. Soon the maintenance man's attitude changed. He let the rest of the young people go inside.

"We'll hold up the sweepings, but you'll have to wait till the rest of the trash is hauled away. Keep back out of the way, please," the policeman warned. "Someone will have to come from headquarters to supervise the job."

For an hour and a half the watchers hung around the entrance as huge container after huge container was emptied into the jaws of trucks and driven away.

"That diamond just *has* to turn up before we go to

the airport!" Barbara said. "We'll die dead if we aren't in on the finish."

"It doesn't look as though there ever will be a finish. Why don't they get going?" Bob moaned.

It was another hour before anyone showed up from the police department. Then, when two men finally did arrive, they were accompanied by three deeply tanned policemen in foreign uniforms. They were quickly identified as the visiting Peruvians. They shook hands with extreme politeness with Trixie and all her friends.

The police promptly busied themselves with searching the sweepings. The Peruvians helped, pawing over every inch of the gigantic accumulation while Trixie ran from one searcher to another, dying to get her own hands on the debris.

After minutes went by, then half an hour, Miss Trask and Mr. Wheeler arrived. Fortunately, Mr. Wheeler was good-natured about the early morning exodus from the apartment. Miss Trask stood quietly aside, watching.

The search continued. Cigarette and cigar stubs, cleansing tissue, burned matches, ashes, crumpled papers, abandoned matchbooks, gum wrappers, old newspapers, magazines—every sort of remnant of a day's activity was examined and pushed aside.

Trixie eyed carefully the ash and dirt residue as the bulkier trash was lifted from it, hoping against hope to catch a glint of the jewel. Her hope was in vain. As careful as Trixie's search was, the Peruvian police were more thorough. Finally, even they gave up. As the last container was carried to a waiting truck the men shrugged their shoulders and admitted defeat.

"It is gone," the spokesman of the group sighed. "It is perhaps Blinky. Or perhaps someone else picked the stone up from the floor. There were many down on their knees searching, no?"

Trixie nodded her head.

"Don't feel so bad, Trix," Mart said. "You did all you could to hold on to it. It looks now like good-bye diamond!"

"Yes, as you say, good-bye diamond," the Peruvian echoed. "At least, Miss Trixie, if we do not find this jewel, we find the other idols and other stolen jewels— maybe. The man who sell this one to you, the police have him, and he has given us what you call a lead, *si?*"

"That's right, Mr. Wheeler," the New York policeman said. "It looks as though we may round up the rest of the loot. I wish I felt confident that we'd round up Blinky, Big Tony, and Pedro. We know they used a black Cadillac while they were in the city, and we've put up roadblocks at all the exits from Manhattan. I feel sorry for the kid who's been mixed up in all this. She might have been in on a sizable reward if she'd had the stone. I guess she'll get something out of it if those two men are caught, for she sure has been on the ball trying to hunt them down!"

"She's a *real* detective. You didn't know that, did you?" Barbara asked the policeman.

"No, I didn't." He winked at Mr. Wheeler.

"My daughter Honey and Trixie work together," Mr. Wheeler said seriously. "They've turned in some pretty hardened criminals. No, I mean it," he insisted as the men standing around him laughed. "I've learned to respect Trixie's ambition. I've an idea you will, too, before this thing is ended."

"Now I've heard everything." The head policeman took off his hat to Trixie. "Well, Miss Detective, you'll have to work a miracle to come up with that diamond now. There's not a clue left. We'll have a full report later," he added, nodding to Mr. Wheeler.

The "Obvious" Answer · 18

A VERY WOEBEGONE group walked single file around the building to the coffee shop.

Inside, they lined up at the long counter. They were studying the menus when Miss Trask, counting noses, asked, "Where's Trixie? Where's Honey?"

"And Jim?" Mr. Wheeler added.

"I thought they went to wash their hands," Diana said, looking around the coffee shop. "They'll probably be here in a minute. We might as well order."

"If anyone is interested in what I think," Ned said, "I'm pretty darned sure that Trixie is off on another scent."

"That's impossible!" Mr. Wheeler exclaimed and slid off the stool. His face was stern. "What could she do now? I'm going to be extremely upset with Jim and Honey, too. That Trixie is indefatigable!"

"Yeah," Mart agreed, "and persistent, persevering, aggressive, resolute—"

"Tenacious, enduring, unfaltering—" Bob added, laughing.

"Unswerving, indomitable—" Mart went on.

"Unflagging," Bob continued without pause, "unflinching, obdurate—"

"And unfailing!" a voice called out triumphantly behind him. They whirled around to see Trixie, who stood grinning, her closed fist above Mr. Wheeler's head.

"Trixie!" They crowded around her.

She opened her hand. There lay the dazzling white diamond, sparkling in the reflected gleam of the ceiling lights.

"Gosh!" Bob cried, awed.

"Wow!" Ned added.

"Where did you find it?" Barbara gasped.

Trixie was so excited she couldn't talk. She started speaking, then sputtered and stopped. Honey came to her rescue. "Daddy, let's go into the lounge, away from this crowd, so we can talk about all that has happened."

"It's fabulous!" Jim said, his eyes on Trixie in deep admiration.

"I found it in the restaurant!" Trixie announced breathlessly. "Right on the floor! Isn't it perfectly beautiful? It was lying there just where the idol fell.

Why I didn't think to look there this morning, I'll never know."

"The obvious always escapes us," Miss Trask said softly. "Where did you actually find it, Trixie? That area had been swept thoroughly. The diamond must have been lodged somewhere."

"It was!" Honey said. "There was a little crevice in the floor. It had fallen into it. When Trixie left the rest of you, Jim and I didn't know what had come over her. We just followed. Then we saw her creep around on the floor and come up with that!"

"Holy cow!" Bob cried reverently. "Now you'll cut in on the reward. The crippled kids sure are lucky to have you for their friend, Trixie."

"And we're lucky to get in on the finish," Barbara said, hugging Trixie.

"Boy, I'll say," Bob added. "Trixie *always* gets her man!"

Trixie's face fell. "Keep the stone for me, please, Mr. Wheeler. You aren't in on the finish, Barbara. I *don't* always get my man, Bob. Blinky, Big Tony, and Pedro are still at large. Worse than that, I don't have the ghost of an idea where they may be."

"Hallelujah for that!" Mr. Wheeler exclaimed. "Let the police take care of them, Trixie. Remember the roadblocks that have been put up."

"I remember that we're working with the slipperiest crooks in the world," Trixie said sadly.

"I'd settle for finding the diamond, Sis," Mart told her. "Boy, you're good—really good! Keeping after that stone till you found it!"

Trixie's eyes brightened at Mart's praise. It never was too plentiful. "Of course I'm glad the diamond has been found. I can just see Blinky's face when he finally grabbed that idol, then got it outside and found the stone was missing! Jeepers, look at the time. I wish you didn't have to take that plane!"

"There's no other way out," Ned said. "It's a good thing we packed our bags last night."

"You haven't had anything to eat!" Diana wailed. "Nobody ate breakfast at that coffee shop."

"Who cares?" Bob spoke for the Iowans. "We'll get something on the plane. I don't know about Ned and Barb, but I couldn't choke a thing down. I'm too excited. Gosh, Trixie!"

"There's never a dull moment around Trixie, Bob. I never thought I'd have a Sherlock Holmes—or should I say Dr. Watson—in my family, either." Mr. Wheeler looked at Honey fondly. "I guess I'd better find some cabs. Is everyone going to the airport?"

"Of course," Trixie said. "If we hurry like everything, maybe there'll even be time to meet the Wellingtons on the plane from Paris."

"That will be simply wonderfully wonderful!" Barbara said blissfully. "Hurry, everyone!"

"Simmer down, Barb," Bob advised. "We'll make it okay. Gosh, just think, those friends of yours were in Paris this morning and now New York for lunch!"

"We'll keep these same cabs," Mr. Wheeler said as they stopped at the apartment. "If your bags are packed, Bob and Ned can pick them up."

"Good!" Trixie clapped her hands. "Then we'll be sure to see the Wellingtons' plane come in. Hustle!" she called to Ned and Bob.

"Before we go back to Sleepyside, we must take the diamond to the police," Mr. Wheeler reminded her.

"And Trix can collect the loot," Mart said.

"We'll have to call Dr. Reed, too," Mr. Wheeler said. "We promised to keep him up to date. Mart, I think you're a little premature about that 'loot,' as you call it. Things don't move that quickly."

Trixie's sparkling blue eyes saddened. "Things probably won't move toward that station wagon at all. Those Peruvian police aren't going to think I've done my work when Blinky, Big Tony, and Pedro are still loose. There are the boys with your bags. Come on. Let's go!"

The cabs sped quickly out the crowded expressway toward Kennedy International Airport in the borough of Queens.

It was a gay and laughing crowd that disembarked, quickly checked the Maine-bound bags, and boarded a bus for the International Arrivals Building. There they huddled together against the rail on the observation deck to watch for a glint of the plane from Paris.

"Oh, I *do* hope it's on time!" Barbara's feet fairly danced. "Did anyone check?"

"I glanced at the board as we passed," Mr. Wheeler told her. "It's on time."

209

"Doesn't it seem as though *everyone* but us is going to some strange place in the world?" Trixie mourned. "See all that crowd down there! See the people in foreign clothes. Look at those Indians, for instance. Look at—great Christopher's aunt! Mr. Wheeler, hurry, hurry—hurry! Police! Police! It's Blinky and Pedro and Big Tony! I'm positive! They're going out to that plane about to take off. Police! Do you see them, Mr. Wheeler?"

"I do," Mr. Wheeler answered. "Here's a policeman, Trixie. Officer! Listen to this young lady and act quickly. It's a matter of vital importance! Thieves are making a getaway!"

The policeman, reacting quickly, called the control tower to hold the plane. Trixie, Honey, and their friends watched, fascinated, as far below them a patrol car roared out to the runway. Uniformed men poured out, surrounded the three thieves, and herded them into the waiting car.

"Jeepers, that's that!" Trixie cried exultantly. "We have the diamond. Blinky, Big Tony, and Pedro are on their way to jail. Now, Mr. Wheeler, we'll see what they have to say at the police station when we go back to the city. . . . Heavenly day, where's the plane from Paris with the Wellingtons?"

"We've missed them," Ned said. "The plane was due several minutes ago. How could we help missing them in all this excitement? But we can find them at the baggage pickup. Boy, is this a day! Stand over there, Trixie, facing the sun. Honey, too. I want to take a picture of the best girl detectives in the United States of America!"

"Don't forget that we almost lost this case," Trixie said modestly. "Why not have everyone in the picture? That means all the Bob-Whites and Mr. Wheeler and Miss Trask. Ned, you'll be the only one missing."

"I don't care about that," Ned said and clicked the camera. "What makes you look so serious all of a sudden, Trixie?" He looked at Trixie curiously.

"The plane's wings shining in the sunlight down there," Trixie answered, "like silver!"

"The last part of the prophecy!" Honey exclaimed. "Oh, Trixie!"

"You're right." Trixie quoted:

> "All is not lost, though, little friend;
> Rejoice, for peril, danger end
> Near silver wings, past river's bend.
> Fortune is yours, fit for a king,
> And hearts of little children sing."

"Wow!" Bob cried. "If that doesn't mean a reward and that station wagon for the crippled children, I miss my guess. Hurrah for the Mexican woman!"

"I hope Trixie and Honey do get a reward, and I hope they can help buy the wagon for the children," Miss Trask said, "but I still say—"

"That it was all a string of coincidences." Trixie finished Miss Trask's sentence. "Maybe you're right, but, jeepers, what if it was? We all had a lot of fun."

"Boy, we sure did," Bob cried. "Our whole visit was tops!"

"It was too wonderfully wonderful!" Barbara sighed ecstatically. "We've had the best time in the whole world! Thanks a million!"

"That goes for me, too," Ned echoed. "Holy cow, Barb and Bob, let's go! We'll miss our plane!"